The Boss Man's Daughters

Lock Down Publications
& Ca$h Presents

The Boss Man's Daughters

A Novel by *Aryanna*

Lock Down Publications
P.O. Box 870494
Mesquite, Tx 75187

Visit our website at **www.lockdownpublications.com**

First Edition February 2017
Printed in the United States of America

This is a work of fiction. Names, characters, places, and incidents either are products of the author's imagination or are used fictitiously. Any similarity to actual events or locales or persons, living or dead, is entirely coincidental.

Cover design and layout by: Dynasty's Cover Me
Book interior design by: Shawn Walker
Edited by: Mia Rucker

Stay Connected with Us!

Text **LOCKDOWN** to 22828 to stay up-to-date with new releases, sneak peaks, contests and more…

Submission Guideline.

Submit the first three chapters of your completed manuscript to ldpsubmissions@gmail.com, subject line: Your book's title. The manuscript must be in a .doc file and sent as an attachment. Document should be in Times New Roman, double spaced and in size 12 font. Also, provide your synopsis and full contact information. If sending multiple submissions, they must each be in a separate email.

Have a story but no way to send it electronically? You can still submit to LDP/Ca$h Presents. Send in the first three chapters, written or typed, of your completed manuscript to:

LDP: Submissions Dept
Po Box 1482
Pine Lake, Ga 30072

DO NOT send original manuscript. Must be a duplicate.

Provide your synopsis and a cover letter containing your full contact information.

Thanks for considering LDP and Ca$h Presents.

ACKNOWLEDGEMENTS

Lord Jesus, I thank you for the gift you've given me by allowing me to put this pen to paper and create. I don't take it for granted. I gotta thank my Beautiful Grumpy Bear, and Heartsong Bear for all the love and support you give me every day. I love you! And to my beautiful Belinda Diane, how do I love thee? Let's count the ways LOL! It would take the rest of my life to put my love to words but I know my actions speak more to you and so I strive to do better every day I LOVE YOU for rocking with me in every way that counts and for showing me restraint when you really wanna show your ass. Your sacrifices are appreciated. I gotta thank my family who supports me. If we struggle together then we succeed together, remember that. I gotta thank each and every one of my fans because I still understand that without you I ain't shit. That keeps me hungry to give you the best of me. I gotta thank my Lock Down Publications Family and affiliates for respecting my grind and believing in my contribution to what you're building. I appreciate it more than you know. Lastly, I gotta thank my haters because you still motivate me as much as you did on my first book. I'm still here, bitch! LOL! LMFAO! As always Aryanna you're the glue that holds me together, I love you beyond words. Special shout out to the real niggas doing numbers behind the G-Wall, keep ya head up because if it ain't life it ain;t long. And if it is life then it's still worth living because your story can keep someone out of your shoes. Each one teach one. Before I go I can't forget my Goon Lawrence, a.k.a Bloody Knuckles, the official Mad Dog. Thank you for teaching me how to see the board, and I'll never forget that summer of lean. LOL!

DEDICATION

This book is dedicated to Thomas Lee Miller because he gave me everything in the form of my beautiful Belinda Diane and because he was everything to her. We love you and miss you, watch over is. Go Cowboys, 11/09/11

Chapter One
Freedom

"Mr. Turner, I just want to be clear with you so there's no misunderstanding, my patience will only last so long. In short, don't bullshit me or insult my intelligence because that'll only piss me off," I warned, taking a seat on the comfortable brown leather sofa next to his daughter.

I could feel her fear radiating from her pores and smell it in her sweat. But if I was in her situation, I might be scared, too. Most people thought they were safe in their own homes, especially white people with a little money, until one day they looked up from their meal at the dinner table to find three bad bitches with guns. One look at the Mossberg Pump I was holding and they knew I wasn't there to sell them Girl Scout cookies, or wolf treats. I meant business.

I may have only been five feet one and a half inches tall with a body full of curves that most niggas wanted to ride, but one look in my eyes told them I was nothing to fuck with. Looking at the heavy set, gray haired man kneeling in front of my sister, I could tell he was beginning to understand this fact, and so was his beautiful wife, who was kneeling in front of my other sister.

To the untrained eye, we probably didn't look like we were 'bout this life, but that's why looks were deceiving. Angel had that movie star beauty with the honey complexion, big brown eyes, pouty lips and disarming smile. We all had that thickness that could make most men cheat, but Angel's five-foot seven-inch height gave her proportions that models envied. Seeing her with that AK-47 pressed to the forehead of the fat man in front of her made me wonder if any model had ever done this.

And Destiny looked just as out of place with her .357 Snub Nose in the eye socket of Mrs. Turner, but only because she was the baby of the bunch and always had a smile on her face. She stood a full inch shorter than me. But because we had the same hazel eyes and chocolate complexion, we could've almost passed for twins, except I rarely smiled. I would have a reason to smile soon if our mission was completed. First, I just had to get the truth out of these nice people.

"P-please, I don't keep cash in the house, but there's jewelry upstairs. Take it," he offered.

"Do you really think I'm here to rob you?"

"Hold up now, Free, this is a nice house and that could be some high dollar shit he's offering up," Destiny interjected.

I knew the stick-up game was her bread and butter, but this wasn't about no money, and I silenced that notion with a pointed look in her direction.

"Mr. Turner, we ain't here to rob you. We're here for information," I said.

"I'll tell you anything just please don't hurt my family," he begged.

"You work for the bureau of prisons in Washington D.C., even though you live out here in Maryland, and the major part of your job description involves the transfer of inmates. My father's name is Johnathan Walker, aka Father God, and he's one of the leaders of the Black Guerilla Family for the east coast. He's doing a life sentence for a double murder, kidnapping, and weapons trafficking. Now because you all know he's Black Guerilla Family he's not allowed to stay in any one prison for more than twenty-four months before he has to be moved again. That twenty-four-month cycle ends in one week, so my question for you is when and where will my father be moved?" I asked.

"I-I don't know that information. We are not told until the date of."

I never understood why people lie when the situation clearly dictates that the truth was the only option on the table.

"Destiny," I said.

Without hesitation, she pulled the trigger and put the late Mrs. Turner's brains all over the nice beige carpet, adding colors that I'm sure didn't blend with the decorator's ideas. As to be expected, the young lady next to me started screaming, but the sound of a shotgun being pumped had the calming effects of a mother rocking her child because she shut right up. I knew she was only seventeen, but her green eyes shown with wisdom, as well as fear, and her survival instinct had definitely kicked in.

"Mr. Turner, I warned you about fucking with my patience. I want you to digest this thought, do you really think we'd be here if we didn't know to be here? Now maybe you weren't that attached to your wife, and I get it because that bleach blonde anorexic type is played out. No offense, Sharon," I said the silently crying girl to my left.

"My point is, if you have any interest in saving your own life I suggest you make that your last lie. Let's try it again, when is the transfer taking place?" I asked calmly.

"I n-need to get to a computer," he murmured.

"Destiny, I believe the man's laptop is in the briefcase by the door, grab that for me. Angel, sit his ass on the couch and stand right over his shoulder where you can watch everything he's doing."

Everybody moved and I got up to look out of the living room window into the night. I was wondering how long we should spend in this house, but the good thing about Mr. Turner having money was that his neighbors weren't close enough to hear shit. Hopefully we wouldn't have to use the big guns until we were leaving, but that all depended on the amount of cooperation we got. It had taken both time and money to get to this point and figure out who had the info I needed, and now that I had my man, I wouldn't be denied.

"Free, the jewelry?" Destiny asked after she'd handed over the laptop.

"Go ahead, but make sure you keep your gloves on and handle that other business to," I said, nodding towards the gas can that had been out of sight by the door.

The average hood nigga would've understood from the jump that no one was walking away from this encounter except me and my sisters. We didn't pull a job without masks and use our real names unless we weren't leaving any witnesses, but selling false hope always helped to keep the process moving along.

"Do your thing, Mr. Turner," I said, motioning towards the laptop with my shotgun.

I could see the sweat mixing with his tears running down his face into the thickness that was his beard. His blue-green eyes were red rounds and fidgety, but I had a hunch that had more to do with his love for Cognac than the stress of the situation. Looking around the living room, I spotted a bar against the far wall adjacent to the fireplace.

"Sharon, go fix your dad a drink," I said.

Slowly she stood on wobbly legs and did as she was told, and I had no objections when she threw back a shot of liquor. She definitely needed it. I hadn't been much younger than she was when my world was flipped upside down, and like her, it all started with my father. I was the oldest out of us girls, which made me my daddy's first, and arguably his most spoiled, but I was also more like him than Angel or Destiny. As far back as my memory could go, I was by my father's side learning and absorbing the education the Georgia school system didn't teach.

What I learned I passed down to my sisters because ultimately it was about survival, and it was a must that all of us survived. I had thirteen years of the street embedded in me by the only man I trusted. But just like anything else, nothing in those streets lasted forever.

"Mr. Turner, I'm waiting, and I don't like to wait," I said, brushing imaginary lint from my black capri pants.

"I-I'm looking for it," he stammered, mashing keys in either a hurry or impatience.

When his daughter came to his side with a full glass of amber liquid, he paused to down half of it without blinking. I could see his nerves lessen visibly. Now all I needed was for that to translate into productive work.

"Sit back down," I instructed his daughter before she got any ideas.

"Yo, Free, they got a safe upstairs," Destiny said, coming back into the living room.

The look she was giving me said she wanted the combination, and we both knew in order to get that she was gonna have to lean on one of the two remaining residents of the house.

"He's busy so asked her," I said, gesturing towards the still shaking Sharon. Destiny's response was to point her gun to Sharon's head and cock the hammer.

"Wait! Th-the combination is 07-16-15," he yelled, pulling his daughter to him in an effort to shield her.

"You got what you need, now go check it out so he can finish what he's doing," I said. Only when Destiny had gone back upstairs did he let his daughter go and turn his attention back to the computer screen.

"Okay. He's scheduled for transfer on the 21st of this month, but it doesn't say where he's going."

"Mr. Turner-"

"I swear it doesn't say where he's going. His destination and transfer time won't be added until later," he replied earnestly.

I looked at Angel and she nodded her head to confirm that the screen was showing the same info he was kickin'. It was good to at least have a date, but the more specific information would've allowed for better planning. We couldn't go at this shit half-cocked or not only could we fail, we'd probably lose our lives in the process. My pops was worth it, but no way that was what he wanted.

Shit, he was going to go off once he heard the plan we were already putting together.

"A'ight, I appreciate your time and cooperation, Mr. Turner," I said, standing up.

"P-Please, I won't tell anyone," he said.

"Oh, I have no doubt," I replied, leveling my shotgun at Sharon's head. I'm not sure what she opened her mouth to say, but the blast from my shot took her head off clean at the shoulders. Simultaneously, I heard the rat-tat-tat of Angels chopper making a meal out of Mr. Turner.

"Destiny, let's ride," I yelled.

"Do you want me to take the laptop with us?" Angel asked.

"Yeah, we need to find out everything we can if we're going to do this right. Dad's been gone long enough. Let's bring him home."

Chapter Two
Destiny

"May I help you?"

"Yeah, Destiny Walker here to visit Jonathan Walker," I said, passing my ID over the counter.

The female guard took it, looked at it, and then went to work on the computer in front of her. My visit was actually going to be a surprise because my dad had no idea I was even in town, but I knew I was still on his visitation list. Anywhere he was he made sure his girl could get to him.

"Have a seat and we'll call you when ready," the female guard instructed, handing me back my ID.

The waiting room was packed. I chose to hold up the wall to avoid my personal space being invaded. From the moment I stepped inside the federal prison gates, I'd felt the hunger of many sets of eyes on me, and it wasn't a feeling I liked. Even with my hair in box braids, a plain, black, long sleeved T-shirt, some black Billionaire Black sweatpants, and some retro Jordans, I wasn't dressed down enough to keep thirsty niggas in their own lane.

I could only imagine what would happen if I came through there looking like money. I probably should've been used to it because niggas in Atlanta acted the same way on the daily, but that was only until they found out my name. My name spoke for itself and mufuckas knew not to come at me like I was pussy. No one knew me up here, but I knew once they saw who I was visiting, they'd wish they kept their eyes in their heads.

I noticed the machine on the wall where you did the money exchange for the debit card that we'd need for the vending machines, and I went to it. Our visit would only be a couple hours, but I still had to feed that big nigga so I put a hundred dollars on the card. After that was done, I went to the bathroom so I could tuck the rest of my cash into a hidden pocket in my panties, figuring that he might need some spending money for something other than commissary.

As soon as I got back to the waiting area, the female guard was waving me through the door that would take me to the back, where I'd be searched. I hated this part because it made me feel like I was the one locked up, but it was necessary in order to get in. I was shown into a tiny room that had a metal table and two metal chairs, one of which was occupied by a short red headed woman. Her face was cute with her tiny freckles and dark green eyes, and her uniform did little to hide that voluptuous body. Different time different place and she might could get what so many men wanted from me.

"Ms. Walker?"

"That's right," I replied.

"Due to your father's high security status, all his visitors are subject to a strip search. Will that be a problem?"

"Well ordinarily you'd have to at least buy me dinner first, but in this case, I'll settle for you telling me your name," I said, walking to the table and sitting on the corner closest to her.

When she looked up at me, her eyes revealed the secret of her naughtiness that she kept hidden just below the surface.

"My name is Kimberlee, but in this setting you can call me CO Klein."

"What about in a different setting?" I whispered, leaning in close enough to smell the cocoa butter on her porcelain skin.

"That depends. You might call me Kim, or KayKay, or Jesus if I'm doing my job right," she replied, standing up and giving me a smile that only increased the wetness between my thighs.

I pulled my T-shirt over my head revealing my matching black sports bra that wasn't doing much to hold my titties down. I was twenty-one and my naked body showed that, without a doubt.

"Hold up," she said, stopping me before I was completely topless.

"I know who your dad is and I'm not about to disrespect you by making you strip."

"You sure?" I asked, flashing her a devilish smile as I stood toe to toe with her.

"Yeah, I'm sure, but this job is only an eight-hour shift. Maybe if you use this we can figure something out after hours," she said, pulling a pen from her pocket and taking my hand, where she wrote down her number.

I liked how bold she was, especially since she knew who my pops was an undoubtedly the reputation he carried.

"I'm wit it," I replied, putting my T-shirt back on.

"Yeah, but can you handle it," she said, licking her juicy lips seductively. Before I had a chance to respond, there was a knock on the door and a male guard asked if she was ready.

"Have a good visit," she told me as I turned and went back out the same door.

I was led to a metal detector and, once I passed through it, I was led down a corridor until we came to a gate. Once I was buzzed through the gate and the metal door a few feet behind it, I stepped into a large cafeteria filled with metal picnic tables. Walking over to the desk at the head of the cafeteria. I told the male CO who I was there to see and he pointed me to an empty table in the far right-hand corner of the room.

I could see the table was empty so I decided to hit the vending machines first and get the preliminary round of snacks and drinks out of the way. No sooner had I gotten everything to the table than I felt him enter the room. It was crazy how one man's physical presence could change the entire atmosphere of the setting, especially when most of these niggas claimed to be the gangsta that my daddy was.

The conversations became quieter and I suddenly found more interest in the cracked linoleum floors than in the man making his way towards me. To the untrained eye, he seemed oblivious to his effect on others, but I knew he knew how uneasy people were around him. He stood six feet five inches and was easily three hundred plus pounds, putting him in the same category with Suge Knight, but more handsome.

He had the complexion of expensive chocolate and a dazzling smile that we all inherited, but most of the time when he smiled it was a warning. Even from a distance, I could see he still had his waves spinning with his hair cut low, and the way his tan uniform molded to him said working out was still his favorite way to pass time. He definitely embodied the phrase 'larger than life', but to me, he was just my daddy.

"What's up, old man?" I said, standing to greet him, and loving the feel of security I always got when he swept me up in his arms.

"What's up with you, Baby Dee? Is everything alright?"

Here I was wrapped up in a smothering bear hug with a man some might consider menacing, but I could hear the fear in his voice. Despite the fact that all his little girls were grown, he still worried about us constantly out there, because he believed the sins of the father would befall his children. The other part was the guilt he felt for leaving us without a mother or a father.

"Everything is fine, dad, we just had to come this way on some business and so I decided to drop in on you."

"We?" he asked, setting me back on my feet and staring down at me.

"Yeah, Freedom and Angel were in town with me."

"And why aren't they here with you now?"

"Because Free is still handling shit and Angel had to get back to Atlanta because she was booked for a party," I replied, sitting back down.

"She still dancing at King of Diamonds?" he asked, joining me at the table as went straight for the barbecue potato chips.

"Yeah, you know she make too much money to quit that shit."

It had bothered him at first that his daughter was a stripper, but one thing he knew about us was that we could handle ourselves. We were all about getting a check and we believed in doing so by any means.

"How is Freedom doing?" he asked.

"You know Free, she is getting to the money and making sure life goes as smooth as possible."

"She must be doing her thing because I've been getting receipts for a thousand dollars every week for damn near a year. My books are strapped."

"Shit, you can have more than that because you know I'm doing my thing, too, but we know Angel is the only one with which it's traceable income, so we don't do too much," I said, pushing a root beer soda his way and taking this fight for myself.

"Smart. You just make sure you and Free are safe out there," he said, leaning across the table so no one could overhear.

There were no lines between us and my father knew that I was putting my robbing game down something serious, and Free was slinging dope a mile a minute. We were raised to depend on no man. We were given all the tools we needed to get to the money ourselves. And we did.

"Daddy, you know, no matter how long we go in between visits, we're all still your kids and we ain't forgot one lesson you taught us about the streets."

When he smiled at me I felt like a little kid at Christmas time and I loved the fact that something so simple still moved me that way. Growing up as fast as we had to, I learned how ugly the world was and how it could change you, which made me understand how precious moments of happiness really were.

"I've missed you, Baby Dee."

"I've missed you, too, daddy, and I'm sorry it's been so long since I came to visit," I said, taking his big hand in both of my smaller ones.

"You know I understand. I mean Maryland is a long way from Atlanta. Speaking of which, how long are you up here for?"

"Well that all depends on Free."

"You said you came up here on business. What do you all got going on?" he asked, leaning closer again.

I hadn't exactly figured out the words I was going to use to explain what we had in mind, but I knew Freedom had sent me because dad wouldn't cuss me out. I was the baby, and even though I was capable of pulling anything off, he'd still know I wasn't the brains behind the operation.

"Right now we're still doing research, but will be ready to handle our business soon," I replied. For a moment, he just stared at me. I thought he might've been looking through me, but I quickly realized I was being sized up.

"What aren't you saying, Destiny?"

"Dad, you can't shoot the messenger," I said cautiously.

"Destiny."

"Fine," I said, looking around to make sure no one was paying attention.

"We all know your two-year transfer is coming up. And this time we want you somewhere different. So, we're taking it into our own hands."

"And what exactly does that mean?" he asked.

"That means pack light. Your time is up and were breaking you out."

Chapter Three
Angel

"Coming to the main stage, the devil's angel!"

I loved my intro because I appeared out of nowhere in a cloud of smoke and focused all the attention in the room on me. With a body like mine there was no need for being shy. I took my time making my way to the end of the stage, knowing how hypnotizing I looked under the flashing red light that was part of my routine. Once I knew I had the crowd, I began my seduction. My body moved like it had a mind of its own and it didn't need the music playing in the background.

I was the seller of dreams and fantasies for both men and women, and the power and that gave me a rush only surpassed by counting my money when it was over. I danced for two songs, the first of which was a striptease involving my red Victoria's Secret ensemble, my double wands, and of course my tail. By song two, all I had on was body glitter and a smile that they'd remember long after they closed their eyes on that night. And just like that, I made a couple grand for ten minutes' worth of work.

If I decided to hit the floor and give lap dances or go to the VIP room, I'd double that, but I was tired after doing a birthday party. One thing about being in Atlanta was when a rapper threw a party, it seemed like every rapper in the city showed up. Of course, that meant big dollars, but it was exhausting having to say no to every nigga who wanted a little 'extra time.' Some bitches went for that, but I sold dreams and not pussy.

I didn't knock the hustle because I'd been on my grind a long time, but it did make it harder on the rest of us dancers who weren't about all that extra shit.

"Angel, what you get into tonight?" Becky asked. Becky with the good hair was something like my partner in crime until it came to the night life.

She was twenty-two years old, like me, and had been on her own since she escaped the clutches of her stepfather at the age of fourteen. A hustler if I ever knew one, standing five-feet, five-inches, caramel complexion, ass and titties so big a bitch knew not to bring their man around her because he would fall in love before the song began. Shawty was a Detroit thoroughbred, but she partied harder than Atlanta's own.

"Girl, I'm tired as fuck so I am looking forward to getting into bed," I replied, sitting at my dressing table to count my money.

"Damn, bitch, you only danced for two songs. I know that ain't enough money to keep you warm tonight."

"You forgetting I did that party today and that was a quick twenty-five thousand dollars. Plus, I got jetlag like of mufucka," I said, yawning hard.

"What did you go up north for anyway?"

"I had to help handle some shit for my pops."

"Bitch, you know your daddy fine as shit right? If he was home I'd be stepmama with the good hair," she said, laughing and flipping her hair.

"Yeah whatever, bitch, you know Free ain't going for no shit like that," I replied, laughing with her.

Freedom was only a year older than me, but she had taken on that mother role when we were kids. When the nightmares came from watching our house burn down with our mother inside, it was Free that held me at night. It was Free that made me and Destiny stay in school, no matter what, and it was her that kept us all together. Most of all, it was her that helped us understand that our father hadn't meant to kill our mother. He hadn't known she was cheating on him, and with one of his rivals no less. And when she'd brought that man into our home to kill my father while he slept, he'd reacted it out of pure survival.

After it was all said and done, he'd tried to keep us from losing both parents so he'd set the house on fire in hopes of destroying the evidence. But in the eyes of the law a man with something to hide is guilty of capital crimes, especially when he already has a target on his back. Dad went to prison, and Freedom shouldered the responsibilities a thirteen-year-old should never know exist. We'd survived ten years under her leadership though, and I trusted no one more in the world.

"You can say what you want to say, but I'll take my ass whooping for some of that dick," Becky said, still laughing, but dead serious.

"Whatever. What you doing tonight?" I asked, tucking the twenty-one hundred dollars into my bra and turning around to face her.

"I don't know, probably get me a few dances and see what's poppin' in the VIP. I need some big bills, for real."

"Well good luck with that," I replied, shaking my head.

"Yeah, I know you don't have that problem, but that's because your ass is stingy."

The truth of the matter wasn't that I was stingy with the pussy, I was just sharing it with myself. I knew it went against every stereotype given a dancer, but I was proud to be a virgin in this day and age. Niggas was always trying to shoplift the pussy or pay for it, but the man who got between these legs would get all I had to give. Until then, I was all I needed.

"Text me so I know you made it home safe," I said.

"I will. You get some sleep and we'll do something this weekend." While she headed out into the club, I quickly changed into some black jeans, a wife beater, and my pink and black Jordan's before going upstairs to holla at the boss.

"Come in," he replied to my knocks on the door. Big Rick, a.k.a. Huggie Bear, ran K.O.D with an iron fist and didn't tolerate any shit from anybody.

If a customer disrespected one of the dancers, Big Rick was known to personally escort them out by their ankles, and the smart ones never came back. The dumb ones learned after they realized they'd always walk with a limp.

"What's up, Huggie?" I said, taking a seat across from his massive red oak desk. He was built kinda like my pops, maybe an inch shorter and his three hundred pounds was teddy bear soft, but his frame was still imposing and he scowled a lot.

"Good set, Angel. You leaving already?" he asked, pausing in his account of the money.

At most strip clubs they did the books and counted by hand, but King of Diamonds was unlike most, which was why Big Rick had a money machine on each side of the computer on his desk.

"Yeah, I'm tired so I'm done early tonight. But I need to Holla at you about my schedule."

"What's wrong with it?"

"Nothing. I just need you to make sure I'm scheduled to work on the twenty-first, but I won't be coming in," I said.

The look he gave me was one of silent evaluation, but eventually he hit a few keys on the keyboard to bring my schedule up.

"You're supposed to be off the twentieth and the twenty-first," he said.

"I know, but make sure it says I'm working all day on the twenty-first."

"Ordinarily, I'd probably bite my tongue off before I say what I'm about to, but you've never made a request like this. What's going on, Angel?"

"Aww, it's sweet that you are worried, but I'm fine. No health concerns or anything like that."

"You just told me to give you an alibi. I'm not worried about health concerns involving you, but I have a feeling that someone else's might be in question," he said.

I knew the look on my face right now what was one void of expression because it was meant to cease any conversation that was inappropriate. Big Rick was cool, but he was also a street nigga, which meant he knew better than to ask certain questions.

"You are scheduled for the twenty-first," he said, shaking his head and hitting a few more keys on the keyboard.

"Thanks Huggie, I owe you one."

"And you know I'm going to collect, too," he replied smiling.

If I were another female, he probably would've been talking about some sort of sexual favor, but he already knew I didn't play that shit. Free had made that clear from my very first day by taking a page from the movie players club and showing up at Rick's house with her Mossberg to discuss that 'pop.' From that day forward, the bar was understood.

"I'ma get out of here, but I'll see you tomorrow," I said, standing up and heading for the door.

"Be safe," he called after me.

I went back down to the dressing room and grabbed my backpack before heading out the side entrance to my car. Most women preferred the attention using the front entrance gave them, and I'd taken that stroll myself a time or two, but tonight I just wanted to be left alone. As I got closer to my silver '08 Rolls-Royce Drophead, I felt the ground moving from the base coming from the system of the two thousand and fifteen Land Rover Range Rover Sport parked next to me. Even in the dark with the trap being black, I still knew who it belonged to, and it only took a moment for him to appear. The driver side door opened, allowing me to clearly hear that OT Genesis bangin' as he stepped out.

"Push it, push it, push it, push it, push it, go get the money, go get the money."

"What are you doing out here, KD?" I asked.

KD was short for King Deuce, and he was one of Free's business associates from Memphis, Tennessee. He was the type of nigga that could get you in trouble in more ways than one because, not only was he a light-skinned pretty boy, he was a hustler who wouldn't hesitate to bust his gun. Not to mention he specialized in the art of what I like to call word vomit. The nigga just opened his mouth and shit fell out that could have a bitch questioning if she'd ever wear panties again. Being that he knew me and my sisters were immune to his charms, he became something like a brother, but Free didn't let that cloud their business relationship because she'd still shoot him if shit didn't go right.

"I was waiting on you. What you think I'm doing out here?" he replied.

"Why didn't you come in or call and tell me to come out?"

"You know why I didn't come in. I don't hit the club when you dance. But I figured you wouldn't be here long because you did that party earlier."

"You keeping tabs on me now?" I asked.

"Not at all, you know some of the homies are in the rap scene down here, so I heard about the party."

Atlanta was definitely small enough for this to be true. It seemed like everybody knew everybody and all their business. It helped to know people who knew KD, though, because he was five deuce Hoover Crip and that meant he had some respek on his name.

"I thought you were in Memphis," I said, sitting on the hood of my car.

"I had to make a run out west to pick up that Belushi and I got back early, so I thought I'd surprise Free."

"She is out of town."

"I know. That's why I came to see you," he replied, smiling.

His ass wasn't slick though because I knew what was behind that smile. Belushi was a mixture of heroin and cocaine that could have a mufucka lit, and since Free wasn't here to take delivery of the shipment, he wanted me to do it.

"Nah, KD," I said, shaking my head.

"Come on, Angel. There's no way I can stay down here, and if I take it with me back to Memphis, Free is going to be dry. You know that's not a good look," he reasoned.

"Mannnn!" I huffed in frustration, seeing my hot bubble bath and bottle of Patron slipping further from my grasp.

"How much is it and where is it?" I asked impatiently.

"Fifty keys and it's right here," he replied, tapping his truck.

"Okay, well you're going to have to follow me to my spot, but turn that damn music down because we don't need to attract any attention."

"Lead the way," he said, climbing back behind the wheel of his truck.

Tossing my backpack on my passenger seat, I got behind the wheel of my own car, cussing Free out under my breath as I led the way to my condo in College Park. While it was true that we were all caught up in the street life in some type of way, I didn't like getting involved in her business. When I came to a stop at a red light, I unzipped my bag, got my phone out, and called her.

"What up, sis?" she asked, answering on the second ring.

"What's up is KD is in town early and you ain't home," I replied, frustrated.

"Shit! Where is he?"

"Behind me, we're on our way to my house. I just wanted you to know that you owe me."

"I do owe you, big time, and we can talk about it when you get here."

"Get where, Freedom? I just got back down here," I replied, seeing my dreams for relaxation completely evaporating.

"Destiny's talk with dad didn't go over too well. We've been summoned to come see him immediately, which means you need to be back out here by tomorrow."

"I told you he-" I stopped talking midsentence as something caught my eye in the rearview mirror. When I gave it my full attention, I felt my stomach drop because, from the looks of it, a long night was about to get longer.

"Oh shit, some niggas are carjackin' KD!"

"Angel you can't let that happen. You gotta do something," Free insisted.

Do something? We were sitting at a fucking traffic light and it was two niggas toting some big shit by way of firepower.

"Man fuck!" I said, reaching into my backpack for the .380 I kept on me.

I had just enough time to put a bullet into the chamber before I saw KD pulled from the driver's seat and shot in the chest at close range. Dropping my phone on the passenger seat, I opened my door and stepped from the car, shooting the nigga climbing and the passenger side first. I hit him twice in the chest, and he fell. Then I dumped four more shots through the windshield, only stopping when it exploded in red.

"KD," I yelled, running to his side and tucking my gun in my jeans.

"I'm good, just help me get in the truck. W-We gotta get out of here," he replied, gritting his teeth in pain. I pushed the body of the would-be attacker out of the truck and helped KD into the driver's seat.

"Can you drive?"

"I'm fine. Just go and I'll follow you," he assured me.

I quickly hopped back into my car and sped off, keeping my eyes on the rearview mirror while searching blindly for my phone on the seat next to me.

"Freedom?"

"I'm here, what happened?" she asked, panicked.

"We're okay. KD is in the truck behind me, but he got shot. I won't know how bad it is until we get to my house."

"I'll have my people meet you there," she replied disconnecting.

My mind raced with questions, wondering how many people had seen what happened and what my next move should be. This particular gun was legal, but two people were still dead. I needed to talk this over with someone because I couldn't afford to make any kind of mistakes. Only one person knew how to handle this though. I needed to talk to my daddy.

Chapter Four
Destiny

"Jesus! Oh, Jesus! I-I-I'm-"

The rest of her sentence was reduced to unintelligible screams as the damn finally broke and the sweetness of her juices gushed into my mouth. I continued to torture her with my tongue while still working my middle finger rhythmically in and out of her tight asshole until I was sure this phase of the storm had passed.

"You're welcome," I said, laying down in the bed next to her.

I could feel her smile of satisfaction through the darkness in the room, but once removed from that environment, she learned really quick who the baddest bitch was in the bedroom.

"I k-know what you were trying to do," she stammered, breathing heavily.

"Oh yeah, and what's that?" I asked, reaching for a piece of melon that came on the fruit platter we'd ordered from room service.

"You were trying t-to make me your bitch."

Now I did laugh out loud, mainly because there was truth in her statement. Any female I went to bed with learned very quickly that there was only one Destiny, and no matter how long they searched afterwards, they wouldn't find a substitute.

"I don't know what you're talking about," I replied, rubbing the melon around her nipple and then following its path with my tongue.

"Fuck!" she moaned on a sharp intake of breath, making me smile harder.

It felt good to release some stress, especially after my visit today. It hadn't gone anywhere near the way I'd expected. I mean, for a minute I actually thought my dad was gonna put his hands on me. To say he was mad was an understatement, but the way he handled it… it still gave me chills. At first, he'd just looked at me like he was waiting on a punch line for a bad joke, but then I saw the change in his eyes. They just went…dead. I didn't feel like he was looking at his baby girl at all, and that was the first time in all my life I'd had that feeling.

Then he'd calmly told me that me and my sisters had forty-eight hours to be sitting in front of him before he stood up and left me sitting there. I knew it was bad, but I didn't know how bad until I'd called and told Freedom what happened. Her response was a silence that I could literally feel, and it gave me goosebumps. So calling Kimberlee and inviting her to my hotel room seemed like a good way to take my mind off of things and relieve some stress.

"You want me to stop?" I asked, letting her ripe nipple slide from in between my lips.

"N-no, I just want you to play fair," she panted.

"What do you mean?" I asked seductively.

She responded with actions by taking the fruit from my hand and giving me the same treatment I'd given her. Normally, I didn't like my titties fondled or sucked, but her hands we incredibly soft and her tongue gave me chills in a different kind of way.

"You like what you taste?"

"I ain't tasted it all," she replied, pushing me flat on my back and climbing on top of me.

I wasn't one who normally gave up control, but I needed this. I could feel my body speaking to hers as her mouth performed magic in the form of lingering kisses. When she got to my clit, my hands found their way into her strawberry mane and I held on as she pushed the door open to ecstasy. She knew what I liked without me telling her because she had her face deep in my pussy, making sure her tongue danced with every inch. I tried not to scream, but the first wave of orgasm hit me so hard I felt my toes crack.

"God-god-goddamnit!" I exclaimed, holding on tighter.

When she brought her fingers into the mix while she nibbled and sucked on my clit, I lost my mind. In twenty-two years, I'd never squirted when I came. But when she took me to the land of milk and honey, I felt might cum shoot out of me.

"I can't, I can't take no more," I whispered, pushing her away and wondering if my legs would ever stop shaking.

I laid as still as I could, listening to her laughter while I waited on my heart to stop beating like death was around the corner.

"N-not funny, bitch," I managed to say, but I had a smile on my face. For once, I actually thought that I'd met my match.

"You thought you were the only one with tongue skills? Oh no, boo, I can hold my own," she said, giving me a teasing kiss that was reigniting the fires below.

"Damn, we taste good together," I said, sucking on her soft, juicy bottom lip.

"Mmm hmmm. Are you ready for round two?" Just as I was getting ready to answer with actions, my phone started going off.

"Hold that thought," I said, grabbing it off the nightstand.

"Can I call you back?" I said by way of answering.

"Nah, we got a problem," Free replied.

"What is it?" I asked, immediately pushing Kimberlee aside and sitting up.

"Some shit went down back home with Angel and Deuce so I'm on my way to the airport now to hop a flight down there."

"What the fuck happened?" I asked, scrambling from the bed in search of my clothes.

"That's a long story that we really don't need to have over the phone. Are you still with the CO bitch?" she asked.

"Yeah, why?"

"Do you think you can get her to get a phone to dad?"

"If that's what needs to happen, then it'll happen," I replied confidently.

"Take care of that, and stay by your phone because I'm gonna call you if I need you back in Atlanta."

"I got you. Be safe and I love you."

"Love you too," she replied, hanging up.

I didn't know everything that was going on, but it had to be bad if she didn't wanna discuss it on the phone, and she was on the next thing smoking out of town. Free wasn't the type to disobey our father, and he expected to see us sooner than later. The only thing I knew for sure was that I wasn't taking my black ass back up there solo to make excuses for them two. You only had to tell me one time that the messenger gets shot for me to learn.

"Is everything okay?" Kimberlee asked.

"I don't know. I need you to do me a favor though."

"What's that?" she asked, smiling and licking her lips.

"I need you to take my father a cell phone."

Her smile vanished instantly and I could see her disappointment at the fact that I obviously didn't mean something sexual.

"I don't do that," she replied.

"What?"

"I don't smuggle shit inside the prison. I have mufuckas asking me to do that shit all the time and I tell them they better find another route."

"Look, I'll pay you to do it. It's not a big deal," I said.

"It's not a big deal to you, but I got a kid to feed at home and I can't afford to lose my job."

I took a moment to put my clothes on while she did the same, and I tried to gather my thoughts so I didn't lose my cool.

"I feel where you're coming from and, normally, I wouldn't push the issue. But this is important and I need you to do it. If you somehow get caught up, I'll take care of you, that's my word," I said.

"I'm sure your word is good, but my answer is still no. I'm sorry."

I didn't say anything I just shook my head. The room quickly filled with an awkward tension filled silence, but Kimberlee was smart enough to get her shit together and make her exit. After waiting about thirty seconds, I grabbed my .38 and followed her out, creeping to my rented black Audi R8 parked in the corner of the Marriot parking lot. I jumped behind the wheel in time to see her burgundy Ford Explorer pull off into traffic.

Even though this wasn't my first time in Baltimore, I still wasn't completely familiar with the landscape, so I made sure to stay no more than two cars back. For thirty minutes, we weaved through the city, until we came to an apartment complex that definitely suggested that she could've benefitted from the extra money I was offering. I watched her park and then disappear into a stairway only to reappear on the second floor.

I parked and waited, wanting to give her time to get in the house and get comfortable, and also give me time to observe my surroundings. There were people scattered everywhere, but no one seemed to be paying me any attention. After fifteen minutes, I tucked my pistol into my sweat pants pocket and got out the car, walking nonchalantly to the building like I'd grown up in that neighborhood. When I got to the door, I knocked, thankful that there were no lights in the pissy smelling hallway in case she wanted to look out the peep hole.

"Who is it?" she called out.

"It's me, Kaykay," I said, hoping that using her nickname would inspire unconscious familiarity. The door swung open, but I wasn't looking into the green eyes I'd expected,

"Who are you?" he asked, looking me up and down from head to toe.

He was a big kid, but I put him at about twelve years old. His hazel eyes spoke directly to his mixed heritage, and right now they were evaluating me the way I'd seen many men do before. He was gonna be a heartbreaker for sure.

"I'm a friend of your moms," I replied, looking past him to the woman approaching us.

Her face was full of questions and unease, but it didn't yet register the fear I knew would come. Before she got to the door I stepped inside, forcing her son to take a couple steps back, but still neither of them understood the danger that was lurking. No doubt it was probably because I had a smile on my face.

"Wh-what are you doing here? And how did you know where I lived?" she asked.

"We need to talk," I said, looking pointedly at her son so she would know this wasn't for his ears.

"Isaiah, go to your room for a minute," she said.

I could tell he was trying to get a read on the situation because he was picking up on his mother's unease, but he had the good sense not to argue or protest.

"What do you want?" she asked when he was out of hearing distance.

"You know who my father is and you know what he's about, so no matter what, there is no escape. I prefer to put in my own work, though. You can do what I say, or die."

Chapter Five
Freedom

Within four hours of all hell breaking loose, I was back on the streets of Atlanta trying to figure out what the fuck happened. I probably would've been able to get information quicker if Destiny was there because jackin' shit was her lane of expertise, but my people would still find out what the deal was. My father had taught me never to believe in consequences, so someone making a move on my shipment had to be investigated like an act of war.

Right now was not a good time for mufuckas to try and be greedy, but when was a good time for that? I'd learned a long time ago that when you get comfortable, you make mistakes. Maybe I was too comfortable. After landing at the airport and making it through security, I picked up my Bugatti 916 from the short-term parking lot. I loved the power and adrenaline that came from riding a motorcycle, plus you rarely heard about mufuckas trying to jack you at a light.

Instead of going straight to Angel's house, I rode past the scene where it all went down, but I didn't stop because the police were still lurking. While I was waiting on my flight, I'd called a few of my niggas to go to Angel's and move the dope, and also to keep guard over her. Once she called to tell me that everything was good and Deuce was sewed up, I made her give me the rundown on how it had all played out. Based on what she said, I figured that whoever it was that came after Deuce had followed him from the club. But had they been there for him or Angel?

The circle of people who knew my connect was small and I trusted them, but maybe that trust had been misplaced. I had too many questions and no answers, which meant I would have to be patient. I hated being patient. Leaving the scene of the crime, I zoomed through the city, making it to Angel's in ten minutes. Angel's condo complex wasn't the type where niggas were scattered around, loitering and doing ignorant shit. You had to have a few dollars to afford rent there.

With that being the case, it wasn't hard to spot the three different cars positioned around the parking lot, but I knew they were there to make sure no one got to my sister or Deuce. Pressing the button to buzz her apartment, I turned my face to the camera in the corner so she could see it was me. Once I was inside, I took the stairs to the second floor and the door was opened before I knocked.

"I'm just glad you're here," Angel said, wrapping me up in a big hug.

"I'm just glad you're okay. I 'bout lost my mind hearing all that happen on the phone and knowing I was helpless to do shit."

"You taught us to handle whatever pops up or pops off so it's all good," she replied, leading me into the house.

The first thing I noticed was my right-hand man, Bone, sitting beneath a cloud of weed smoke in the living room with a blunt in one hand and a Mac-11 in the other. His six foot one inch, two-hundred and fifty-pound frame looked relaxed, but I knew how alert he always was. Bitches looked at him and saw a chocolate pretty nigga, but he was lethal and unapologetic about it. Above all else, he was loyal.

"What's good, bruh?"

"Everything's straight," he replied, extending the blunt my way.

I wanted to indulge and unwind a little, but I needed a clear head to make sense of the shit that had happened.

"Later for that. Where is everybody?" I asked.

"At the main house taking care of business like you wanted. We sent the young niggas out to put their ears to the streets and everybody else is getting back to the money."

"Those Deuce peoples down in the parking lot?" I asked.

"Yeah, they wanted to keep eyes on him up here, but you know Angel ain't going for having a bunch of niggas in her house."

"I damn sure ain't," she chimed in.

"Where's Deuce at?" I asked.

"He's in the back in the spare bedroom. I got Becky sitting with him until the pain medication kicks in."

"How bad was it?"

"From what the chick who stitched him up said, the bullet went straight through his shoulder and he's gonna live," Angel replied.

"Good thing you actually knew a dancer who's putting herself through medical school," Bone said laughing.

I shook my head at his comment and made my way towards the back to check on King Deuce. It didn't surprise me that he'd come away from this with nothing more than a new scar because the nigga had more lives than any alley cat. I'd known him before he was King Deuce, all the way back to when he was called Baby Deuce in the streets and Vontae by his momma. I knew the hell he came from on the streets of Memphis, and that it took a special kind of luck to make it out alive. He'd definitely pushed that luck to the limit, though.

"You gonna make a mufucka kill you," I said, opening the door to Angel's spare room, but I couldn't finish the rest of the sentence because what I was seeing was unreal.

Here I was worried about this nigga being shot in my city with my dope, no less, and he was in here with Becky riding his dick for all it was worth. Most people would've stopped when someone unexpected entered the room, but not Becky.

"G-give us a m-m-minute. I'm almost d-done," she moaned, looking back at me while she rode him faster.

"Trifflin," I replied, closing the door and going back to the living room.

Angel had a nice place, two bedrooms, one and a half baths, good sized kitchen and dining room, and a comfortable living room, but it wasn't big enough for me and Becky with the good hair. That bitch would become Becky with the bald spot quick. I tried to tolerate her because she was Angel's friend, but what type of renegade bitch was worried about getting a nut from a nigga that had literally just got shot? And she was taking the pipe raw. I knew Deuce, and calling him a whore was an understatement.

"Has he finally passed out from all those pills yet?" Angel asked.

"Nah, I think your homegirl slipped him a little blue pill."

"A little blue pill? Tell me they're not in there fucking right now."

"That's your friend," I said, disgusted.

"I should've known better, bitch said earlier she needed some dick."

"Yeah, well if her pussy is the thing that kills his ass, I imagine his crew is gonna give her all the dick she can handle," I replied, sitting next to Bone on the couch. He hadn't stopped laughing since I'd told them what was going on.

"Messy females, I can't stand," I said, taking the blunt this time when he offered it and filling my lungs with smoke.

"Shit, that nigga almost died tonight, he deserves to get his rocks off," Bone said.

"If I was him, I'd be worried about who tried to rock me. I mean, thank you, though, my nigga. That shipment is early so if it was some competition laying in wait, they'd still be waiting."

"True."

"So, who do you think it is?" Angel asked.

"I don't know, but it's either somebody in his crew or just some niggas wanting his truck," I replied, hitting the blunt again and passing it to Angel.

"You know it's only a matter of time before the police show up here, right?" Bone asked.

"Why do you think I wanted the dope gone ASAP?" I replied.

"We didn't come straight here, though. I took him to get sewed up, and when she was done, I told her to get going for a while. I gave her twenty-one hundred dollars and she'll call if she needs more, but hopefully by then we've come up with the plan," Angel said.

I hoped she was right, but the reality was that she'd shot two people who weren't posing an immediate threat to her. One thing was for damn sure, she was going to need a good lawyer.

"We need to call a lawyer as soon as the sun comes up," I said.

"We needed to get in touch with dad," Angel replied, passing the blunt to Bone.

"I got Destiny working on that. Luckily for us, she decided to fuck one of the COs that works at the prison, and I called her and told her we needed to get a cell phone inside. I couldn't get into details, obviously, but she knows shit got real out here."

"You said we got summoned to come see him. Was he big mad or little mad?"

"From what Destiny said, he was big mad, but I don't understand why. I mean, I know he's gotta be tired of being caged in," I replied, noticing Becky walking up the hallway.

"Bitch, what's wrong with you?" Angel said shaking her head.

"Don't judge me bitch, I told you I needed some, and shot or not, that nigga is fine. Plus, have you seen his dick?"

"Nah, he's family and we don't get down like that."

"Girllll, let me tell you-"

"We got shit to handle and I'm sure you two can swap stories later," I replied, trying not to get ignorant with that hoe.

Becky looked at me for a split second like she wanted to say something, but she swallowed her comments and hid behind a fake smile. Smart girl.

"Well, I'ma get out of here, Angel, but call me if you need me and tell KD I said bye," Becky said, making a fast exit.

"You so mean," Angel said, laughing, once the door had closed.

"Yeah, whatever. Deuce, bring your ass out here," I yelled, unwilling to walk back into the funk of their escapades.

My phone was vibrating from a text message so I dug in my pocket to see who it was from at this time of night.

"Destiny said dad will have a phone in four hours when the CO goes to work," I said, already texting her back.

"So, what's the plan?" Angel asked.

That was a good question because I needed to decide on the order of operations. Eventually, Angel was gonna have to turn herself in to avoid looking guilty. But I couldn't let her do that without being sure she'd get a bond. I fully intended to hear what my father had to say, but in the end, his ass was still coming up out of there. I needed both of my sisters by my side to make that happen, though.

"We can't have you looking like you're on the run, but you being inside right now ain't an option," I said.

"You know I ain't gonna let her get jammed up, homie," Deuce said, coming into the living room and putting his arm around Angel's shoulders.

He didn't have a shirt on, just some blood-stained jeans, and I could see the redness around the gauze that was taped to his chest high on his left shoulder.

"Good to see you're still alive, my nigga," I said, smiling despite my disapproval of his hoe tendencies.

"Thanks to my Angel here. You know a nigga like me don't speak pig Latin, but for her I'll let the cops know what the business is."

"That'll help, but they still gonna be looking at her sideways because the niggas weren't trying to jack her and they didn't threaten her with a gun," I replied.

"The point is them niggas had guns and I got shot, so what was she supposed to do, get out of the car and say please stop? They would've blown her shit back. So, it was either let me die or do something about it, and I don't got no jury convicting her on this."

His argument had some valid points, but I wanted hear that out of the lawyer's mouth before we made a move either way.

"I was thinking I could call Darnell," Angel said slowly.

I knew Darnell was a cop from Atlanta P.D. that was always at the club tricking off his little check on lap dances. From what I'd heard, he liked to pay to play a little bit, too. But there was a big difference between buying some ass and turning a blind eye to murder.

"Nah, that's not the move we're gonna make. We'll talk to dad first. Deuce, do you think it was anybody you know?"

"Their faces weren't familiar, but they were young, though. I know the police gotta identify the bodies, so once I know their names, I can find out more. Swear to god, though, Angel handled her business," he replied, smiling down at her.

"Of course, she did, nigga, she's my sister. Look, we got til six a.m. before we make our next move, so everybody needs a couple of hours of sleep because it's guaranteed to be a long mufuckin day."

"You ain't gotta tell me twice," Deuce replied, kissing Angel on the top of the head and retreating the way he came.

"I'm too wired to sleep," Angel said.

"I know, sis, but you gotta try, at least. The odds are good that we're gonna have to go see dad and you wanna be rested for that."

She knew I wasn't lying to her and she didn't offer up any more protests.

"What do you need me to do?" Bone asked.

"I need you to handle the business while I focus on this other thing with my pops. Make sure all fifty keys are distributed equally through our traps, and I want you to personally make the pick-ups of the money."

"You really gonna break him out?" he asked, rolling another blunt.

"I got to. We need him."

I never minded shouldering the responsibilities of taking care of my sisters, especially since I didn't want them to end up in foster care. At thirteen, I'd had no choice but to become something like a mother, and in the last ten years, I felt like I'd lived a lifetime. I didn't have any regrets, but I was tired. I wanted things to go back to how they were when I was daddy's girl and he made sure everything was alright.

"I can handle the business, and you know that. You just make sure you know what you're doing and you make it out of that situation alive."

We spent another hour going over the business details before he left to get shit in order. Once he was gone, I fixed myself a shot of henney and laid down on the couch to rest my eyes for a second. The next thing I knew, Angel was shaking me awake.

"Free, your phone keeps ringing, answer the damn thing already."

I picked it up off the coffee table and looked at a number I didn't recognize.

"Hello?"

"All three of you get your asses up here now," he said. I didn't get a word in before he hung up in my ear.

"Get a shower because we gotta go. He's definitely big mad."

Chapter Six
Freedom

I lived in a generation of nicknames. It was rare that you ever heard a nigga using his government name, and females had picked up on the trend, too. But that was mainly because mufuckas was 'bout that life. We couldn't make it too easy for the cops to track us down when shit hit the fan. One of the things I'd learned at my father's feet was that in his day your nickname was something you earned, something you put work in for, because only then would the reputation behind that name be respected. When Birdman said "put some respek on my name," he knew what he was saying because he was an old-school street nigga.

My dad's nickname was FatherGod, and I knew that came from both his lack of mercy at times, as well as his willingness to let someone pray before they met their end. A lot of lessons I'd learned through him and with him while my sisters had gotten the translation from me. I'd seen how brutal and cold-hearted he could be, but it was never without reason or provocation. What all of this meant was that I knew him in a way that my sisters never could, which gave me the ability to see him in a way they couldn't. From the moment he stepped foot in the visitation room, I knew it was FatherGod walking towards us, and not simply my daddy.

"Neither of you say shit, let me talk," I whispered under my breath.

I made sure to look at them both in the eye to make sure they understood, and the fear I saw in their eyes told me they did. If I hadn't picked up on in the look on his face as an indicator that he was feeling some type of way, the fact that he didn't ask any of us for a hug before he sat down made shit clear. His penitentiary gaze found Destiny first, and then Angel before finally stopping on me.

"Speak. And don't think about feeding me no bullshit either," he commanded.

"Wouldn't dream of it. Where should I start?" I asked calmly.

"Start with what happened last night," he said.

I had to resist the urge to look at either Destiny or Angel, but the more I thought about it, the more I knew they hadn't been the ones to tell him. He may have been a resident of the state of Maryland, but his heart belonged to Georgia, and Atlanta was in his veins. I had always known that he kept tabs on us, I just didn't know he could be brought up to speed so fast. We were sitting in the back of the cafeteria with no other visitors or families around us, but I still checked my surroundings before speaking.

"Some niggas tried to carjack one of my associates and he was in the process of delivering a shipment to me."

"If he was delivering a shipment to you, why was Angel the one caught up in the bullshit?" he asked.

"Because he was early and I was still up here. Angel called me and told me what was going on, and while we were on the phone, the shit went down."

"Angel, why did you get out of the car?"

"Because I told her to," I replied before she could speak. The brown in his eyes seemed to get darker for a second.

"I was talking to Angel," he said just above a whisper. His change of tone caused the hair on the back of my neck to stand up and salute.

"KD is like family, daddy, I couldn't just let them niggas kill him like that," Angel said.

"So you decided that dropping two bodies on a public street was the best thing to do?" he asked.

"No, but it was the only thing to do. And he would have done the same for me," Angel replied.

My sisters probably didn't notice the slight change in our father's demeanor, but I did because I knew how much he respected loyalty above all else. Knowing his children lived life the same way was something he could never argue against.

"You talk to the cops?" he asked.

"Free said to get a lawyer first."

"Is your friend gonna do the right thing?" he asked, turning his attention back to me.

"He is still in Atlanta waiting on us to get back so we can handle everything. I retained a lawyer during the flight out here and we're supposed to meet her this evening when we get back," I replied.

"That's good. The sooner it's handled, the less it looks like she was trying to get away with something. What about the gun that was used?"

"Clean and legal pops, and I'll give it to the lawyer when I turn myself in," Angel said.

I saw him visibly relax, and when he grabbed a bag of barbecue chips from the assortment we had on the table in front of us, we all breathed a little easier. So far, we'd avoided getting our heads blown off, but I knew what was coming next because I followed his eyes as he took in what we were wearing. Coming into the situation, we knew to dress down and for comfort, and not to wear shit the administration could complain about.

With that in mind, each of us decided on denim Black Billionaire jeans, Air Max, and T-shirts. The catch was that all of our T-shirts had a huge picture of him with the words 'free our father' across them. Mine was white, Destiny's was gray, and Angel's was blue. It was my idea to wear these shirts so he'd get my message loud and clear.

"Let's move on to the next topic," he said, eating his chip slowly.

"I take it you have a problem with our plans, but I don't understand why," I said honestly.

"Why? How about because the odds of that shit happening without you getting killed or caught is beyond slim. That's just some reckless shit."

"You know me better than to think I'd come at a situation this serious without using my satellite. You didn't raise no dummies, dad, so what's really the issue?" I asked.

At first he didn't answer, he just kept chewing while looking from one of us to the next and back again. Even knowing him as well as I did, I didn't know what was running through his mind in the moment, especially since I expected happiness when I first thought of the idea.

"Why now?" he asked.

"Daddy, I wanted to do this the first day you were taken away from us, but I knew something like this would take money and power. I always figured you had your reasons for not asking your homies to get you out, which meant it had to be us. We finally got the money and power," I said.

"I did have my reasons," he replied softly.

I could see sadness in his eyes that I'd never seen before. My father was a man who displayed few emotions, and I knew that was in part because of his definition of what a gangsta was. Him coming into his own as a man was done on the streets of Atlanta, but the first twelve years of his life were molded and defined by the streets of Chicago. Growing up in Chicago, gangstas didn't cry, they didn't even feel because it would lower one's life expectance in a major way. As a result, I didn't see a lot of vulnerability in my dad, but sometimes the window would open and a breeze would blow back the curtain so I could catch a peek.

"What were your reasons dad?" I asked. He took his time finishing up his chips before taking a swig of his soda, obviously gathering his thoughts.

"My guilt," he replied shortly.

Hearing that word spoken from his mouth made me look at my sisters to see if they were wearing the same confused look I was. They were.

"What are you talking about dad?" I asked.

"Prison gives you time to think. For the last ten years, I've had nothing but hours and days and months to look back at my life and the decisions I've made. That type of uninterrupted time can swallow a man with regrets or it can bring you moments of clarity. I found clarity because I can see now that my relationship with your mother was fucked up before that night when shit went wrong."

I don't think any of us expected this conversation to detour into our mom. I mean that was more or less a topic of discussion none of us went near, and especially not with our dad present. We each chose to hold onto the better memories we had of her and block out the fact that she gave it all up for greed and a nothing ass nigga. I never knew whether she thought it was love, but being a veteran in the same streets, I knew that nigga hadn't loved her.

"Every relationship has problems, but she still didn't have to do what she did," I said.

"I could've done shit differently too, sweetheart, and that's what I've learned in all these years. Maybe if I had done things different, or loved her more, then-"

"Dad don't. 'What if' gets you nowhere, and that train of thought is for suckas," Destiny said.

"We loved mom, but she made her decision and that decision cost us two parents. We can't get her back, but we can bring you home," Angel said.

"We need you, daddy," Destiny said sincerely.

"You don't need me, you just think you do. You girls have grown into beautiful, independent young women and you did that by having each other's back. Free can-"

"I ain't you," I said.

"We've done what you said and we held our own in the streets, but I ain't you and this family ain't whole without you. We need you home," I told him, seeing my sisters nodding their heads in agreement.

I could tell he was considering our words, which at least meant he wasn't dismissing us off hand. No nigga in his right mind wanted to be stuck in the box, but a lot of them found solace in knowing that one day their time would be complete. My father didn't have that comfort because a life sentence in the feds meant he was only coming home ten toes up. Deep down, he didn't want to spend his last days like this, and I'd be damned if I allowed it.

"You can't pull this shit off right now. Your window of opportunity is still too small. My two years is almost up and-"

"Your two years is up in five days and they'll be transferring you that following Monday," I said.

"Do you know that for a fact?" he asked.

"You know I always do my homework before I go outside to play," I replied, smiling and thinking about how he used to make me do just that when I was growing up.

It had always been a sore subject with him that I didn't finish school, but school didn't pay, and that was the reality of the situation I had to take on. I felt like somehow Angel and Destiny graduating high school made up for it though.

"Is your plan a solid one?" he asked.

"Nothing is perfect, pop, but we got this," Angel replied.

"First things first, you've got to handle your situation before you all can even think about the crazy shit you're talking. Deal with that, and then we'll see."

I couldn't hide my smile because I knew my father well enough to know that we won him over. The only thing left to handle now was making sure Angel didn't go to jail in the immediate future, and I was already thinking of an insurance plan to make sure that didn't happen. With the business conversation out of the way, we fell into our relaxed rhythm of just kickin' it. All of us knew the face our father had to present to the general population, but this was his time to let his guard down and be human for a little while.

Sometimes I even caught the guards looking in our direction when they heard him laugh because it was so foreign to them. Soon he'd be able to laugh and live without having to look over his shoulder, and he'd reclaim all that he'd lost. The streets had better pray because Father God was definitely coming.

Chapter Seven
Angel

I have never known the type of exhaustion my body was feeling at this moment. I felt like I'd literally been on the running for the last two days. But as much as I wanted to sleep, I knew there was still so much to do. It had been wishful thinking that my nap on the plane would somehow rejuvenate me because before my drool had time to dry on the first-class pillow, we were landing. Now here I was walking into my apartment wanting nothing more than to crawl underneath my bed, yet knowing that wasn't even a possibility.

"Are you serious right now?" I said, stopping just inside my doorway at the site of Becky trying to swallow KD's dick whole.

"M-my bad, I didn't think you'd mind," he replied, grabbing a fistful of her hair so she wouldn't get any ideas about stopping.

"Whatever," I said, closing the door and going to my bedroom.

I made sure to lock my bedroom door before stripping naked and going to my closet to find something to wear. Free had told me to present myself as the virginal hero that I was, so I chose a cream Zac Posan pantsuit with some matching five inch heels. Underneath, I only had on my Victoria's Secret black laced bra. I mean, yeah, I was a virgin, but I liked to look naughty, and that would help if the cops were guys. I sold dreams all day long, why should today be any different? After I had my clothes laid out on my queen sized bed, I went into my bathroom and turned the shower on, not even waiting for it to get hot before I jumped in.

I hadn't realized how tense my body was until I felt myself relaxing beneath the pounding of the water spray. Without warning I felt a pounding and a throbbing somewhere else, alerting me to the fact that, in the midst of all the chaos, I'd neglected myself. I wasn't like most females, I needed complete privacy to cum, and there was no time like the present. As soon as my fingers touched my clit, I felt my body come alive, hungry and demanding satisfaction. I had to brace myself against the shower wall with my right hand because I had the middle finger of my left submerged and drenched inside me, while my thumb danced with my clit.

The first wave was like a tsunami, lifting me up on my tippy toes as I fought the scream trying to rip itself from my throat. I'd heard women talk about dick like it was the second coming of Christ, but no man would ever know my body better than me. Proof of that happened when I changed directions of how I was rubbing my clit while sticking my finger deep inside my still throbbing pussy. Immediately, a hurricane ripped through me and my orgasm forced me to my knees right there on the shower floor.

I felt like I was under water with the way I was gasping for breath, but I could hear and feel my body singing like the weekend. I damn sure deserved it, and I earned it. It took me a few minutes to peel myself off the floor and stand on wobbly legs, but I felt better in every sense of the word. Something about getting a nut cleared your mind of all other bullshit and gave you focus. Made me wonder if actual sex had the same effects. It took me fifteen minutes to wash my ass and another ten minutes to get dressed, and by the time I walked back into my living room, the freak show was over.

"Where's Becky?" I asked.

"On to the next one, I guess. I told her we had shit to handle and I'd holla at her later. Maybe."

"You ain't shit," I said, laughing and pulling my phone out so I could shoot the lawyer a text. Surprisingly, Freedom had trusted me to handle everything while she made her rounds, and Destiny was gonna meet me at the police station whenever that time came.

"What did you find out while we were gone?"

"Nothing really. It was two young niggas that been getting mufuckas from Bankhead to here, and everything in between," he replied, pulling his T-shirt over his head and stepping into some new blue and white Jordan's.

"I don't know. That don't sound like the whole story. I mean, who goes for a Range Rover when you've got a Drophead Rolls in front of it?"

"Yeah, but everybody knows who that Drophead Rolls belongs to, homie, and you know niggas ain't that stupid. I'm coming through the city with some fly shit and I got out of town tags."

"True shit," I said.

"We need to get this all situated, though, because I gotta get back to Memphis and handle business."

"How's the shoulder feel?"

"Hurts like a mufucka, but it'll heal. You got a lawyer?" he asked.

"The best in the city. We going to meet her now, you wanna follow me and your truck?"

"Nah, not really, but it's best that I do in case the cops got any questions. I made sure to tell my niggas to put plastic down, not to clean it," he said.

"A'ight, let's go then."

The lawyer had sent me her address so I typed it into my GPS on the way downstairs to my car. Before we left, I made sure I had my carry conceal permit, gun license, and receipt for the purchase of my gun because I didn't want no disputes about my shit being legal. With everything tucked into my purse, I headed downtown into the business district. On a weekday, it would've been packed down here, but it was a damn ghost town and that told me that Free must've kicked some serious bread at this bitch. Her name was Miranda Sorenson and she had a reputation of being Johnny Cochran with a vagina.

I don't know if she was good enough to get OJ off, but she damn sure better keep me from doing a bid. Her offices were on the fourth floor of a shiny building, and I texted her from the parking lot to let her know we were on our way up. When she met us in the hallway, my first impression was that she could be a dancer easily. We were about the same height and the plum colored suit she had on did not a damn thing to hide her curves. Her skin was what I'd probably call mocha, and it was flawless. I couldn't even tell how old she was.

"I'm Miranda," she said, extending her hand.

"Damn," KD mumbled loud enough for me to hear.

"Nice to meet you. I'm Angel and this is Vontae."

"The pleasure is all mine," KD said, pushing me out of the way to make sure Miranda got the full effect of his smile and presence. It wasn't gonna take long before the word vomit came out in full force.

"Follow me to my office," she requested, leading us through a frost covered door that read "Miranda Sorenson Attorney at Law."

Directly behind the door was a receptionist desk shaped like a horseshoe with a wall of about ten chairs to the right, which served as the waiting area. The color scheme was lavender mixed with deep purples and black scattered throughout, but the feeling it gave off was inviting. To the left was a hallway with several doors on each side and it was this way that we were led, entering the first door on our right.

From the jump, I could tell this was where shit got real because her office was decorated for function and not to give you the warm and fuzzies. There was enough chrome and metal as to be confused with an operating room. Her desk was glass, and even though the swivel chair behind it looked comfortable, the two-black low back leather chairs in front of it didn't give the same illusion.

"Please, have a seat," she said.

"I saw the reports about the shooting this morning on the news soon after your sister retained me, but I need you to walk me through what happened."

KD and I both recounted what had gone down while she listened attentively, never once interrupting, only shaking her head.

"Did you bring the gun and all of its paperwork with you?" she asked.

I pulled everything out of my purse and sat it on her desk, making sure the gun was cleared and the clip empty. Before she touched anything, she reached in her desk drawer and pulled out a pair of latex gloves along with a large Ziploc bag. After she put the gloves on, she began a slow, methodical examination of the gun and all the relevant documentation. When I looked over at KD, I could tell he was watching her as closely as I was, but I knew it wasn't for the same reasons.

"What's our next move?" I asked after enduring several minutes of silence while she studied my paperwork.

"Well, if everything played out the way you said it did, and I'm betting the traffic cam footage will corroborate that, then we should get a favorable deal from the district attorney."

"Deal? You mean like me having to go to prison?" I asked, already mentally arranging my travel plans to leave the country.

"No, I won't agree to any prison time and the D.A. is smart enough to know no jury would send you to prison either."

"Told you," KD said.

"The fact still remains, though, that you killed two people and you can't walk away from that without some type of consequence. Both of you coming forward allows you to get in front of this and gives me leverage to negotiate," she said.

"And what is it exactly that you're gonna try and negotiate for me?"

"I'm thinking two counts of involuntary manslaughter as the worst case scenario with a suspended sentence and probation," she replied.

I didn't like the idea of having a criminal record because it fucked with my squeaky-clean image, but I knew she was right about not walking away from dropping two niggas scot free.

"So, what's our next move?" I asked again.

"Right now, I need to make some calls," she said, putting everything I'd given her into the Ziploc bag and sealing it before popping her gloves off and reaching for the phone.

It took her thirty minutes, but she managed to have a tow truck come for KD's truck, and get the D.A to come in on a weekend evening to meet us at the police station. I couldn't lie, I was impressed, and I liked the confidence she maneuvered with because it meant she wasn't gonna just let the law run over me.

"How long will they have my truck?" KD asked frustrated.

"It shouldn't take more than a few days," Miranda replied.

"I gotta get back to Memphis," he said, looking at me so I'd get the message about the business he had to handle.

"You can take my car, but you know that's your ass if you fuck it up," I warned.

"Sistergurl, you know I got you," he replied smiling devilishly.

"Ms. Sorenson, when we go to the police station, will I be arrested?"

"No. You'll be booked and processed, but I'm hoping to get you released on your own personal recognizance, or with a very low bond," she replied.

As long as I didn't have to spend a night in jail, I was good. I pulled out my phone and sent Destiny a text to let her know that she didn't need to meet me at the station, she could go to the bail bonds and have him ready in case I needed him. When I was done with that, I sent Free a text and let her know everything that was going on, and told her to forward it to dad so he wouldn't worry.

"A'ight, Ms. Sorenson, how do you wanna do this?" I asked.

"Just follow me in your car to the station and I should have you back home before the ten o'clock news comes on."

"How 'bout you let me take you for a late dinner when this is over, just to say thank you for all your hard work?" KD suggested to Miranda.

I started to say something, but I bit my tongue and shook my head because I didn't wanna cock block. True shit, this nigga thought he was an R&B singer because he would try to shake a bitches panties loose anytime anywhere. Miranda hadn't said anything yet, but I could see the lust in her eyeballs and it was hard not to laugh. The text I got back from Destiny wiped the smile off my face, though. We had a problem, and it wasn't one we needed.

Chapter Eight
Destiny

"Please! Please, I've told you everything I know."

"You know, that's what they all say until something jogs the memory," I replied, looking down into the swollen face of the man strapped to the table.

He actually wasn't technically strapped down. His head was just locked in a vise that was attached to the table. I bet he was rethinking this addition to his work station right about now. Sandman owned the number one chop shop in all of Atlanta, and he didn't deal in junk, so it was only natural that I come to him about whoever tried to jack Deuce. Normally, I had a good relationship with Sandman, he'd treated me fairly when boosting cars had been my meal ticket.

These days, I spent more time robbing niggas who were in direct competition with Free, which meant Sandman and I didn't have a lot to talk about. I stil didn't feel like that was a good enough reason to lie to me, though. Me and my nigga, Big Baby, had come here with civilized intentions, but the moment Sandman let it slip that the shit that went down with Deuce wasn't an accident, I knew things were gonna go bad. Big Baby was six foot two inches, two hundred and ninety pounds of muscle with skin so dark you could only call it a mean kind of black.

Just his looks alone were enough to scare a mufucka, but when you added in the fact that he didn't talk, that only upped the fear factor. Still, not his presence or even the subsequent ass whooping was enough to make Sandman talk. It was just me, him, and Big Baby all alone in his warehouse, which was far enough down a side street that he'd lose his voice from screaming before anyone ever heard him. The location was perfect for torture, but I didn't have the time, which meant I had to go from A to Z and skip all letters in between.

"Tighten him up one time," I said, watching the beige of his skin tone get redder across his forehead.

Sandman was six feet, about two hundred and fifty pounds, and he was old school, so I knew he wasn't no bitch, but he had to know I was way too much of a bitch for him.

"Who ordered for King Deuce to get jacked and shot?" I asked again.

"I-I don't know," he cried, trying in vain to free his head from the clutches of the vice.

"Big Baby, see if you can find me some bleach or rubbing alcohol around here. Check the bathroom," I suggested, leaving Sandman fighting his helpless fight while I went in search of the tool I had in mind.

I could've always just shot him, but where was the fun in that? I found what I was looking for and returned to Sandman just as my phone started vibrating in my pocket. It was Angel, and although she was giving me good news, I had to give her the bad by telling her that Deuce getting jacked wasn't a coincidence. I promised to fill her in once I had the details. I sent Free a text and told her to call the bondsman because I was in the middle of some shit I couldn't get out of. I knew she'd understand and wouldn't ask any questions.

"That'll work," I said, taking the bottle of Clorox bleach from Big Baby and sitting it at my feet.

"I think I've been more than patient with you, Sandman, and I did that because we go back a long way, but you are making this hard on yourself. Deuce is like family to me, and you know we support our own."

"D-Destiny, please! All I can tell you is that you and your sisters don't need to get involved in this shit. It ain't got nothing to do with you."

"Last time I'm going to ask nice, who's behind it?" I asked, showing him the box cutter I picked up off of his workbench. His crying intensified, but he didn't utter a word.

"Maybe you can't see what I'm holding through that swollen eye. Let me help you," I offered, placing the blade on top of his eyelid and then dragging it across with a surgeon's precision.

His screams were high-pitched and long, but they served as motivation instead of the deterrent he probably wished they were. I kept cutting, despite his screams, until his eyelid was nothing more than loose skin. Then I snatched it off with my fingers. I didn't think his screams could get any higher than they were at this moment, but I was prepared to put that theory to the test. I picked up the bleach and poured some of it into the cap before dumping it straight into his bloody eye socket. The aroma of bleach is powerful, but it didn't cover up the smell of shit that was suddenly floating in the air alongside his gurgling screams.

"Bet that hurt, huh? The fucked up thing is that you got two eyes, which means twice as much pain. You know what I always wondered? What would a face look like with no lips?"

"Monster," he screamed, flopping around like a fish.

"It's not nice to call people names, and I resent being called a monster because I'm just doing what I gotta do. See what I'm saying? Ooops, that was a poor choice of words considering your blind in one eye," I said laughing.

"I-It was Monster. Monster did it," He yelled in agony.

"Who the fuck is Monster?" I asked, looking at Big Baby. His response was to shrug his shoulders and shake his head.

"Who's Monster, Sandman?"

"Hoover, Hoover that's in Nashville. He wants King Deuce dead and that's all I know. Destiny, please," he begged, still trying to fight his way out of the vice grip.

I've never heard of this nigga Monster, but there was no reason I should have because we didn't have nothing in common, except

King Deuce. Me and my sisters weren't into the whole organized gangs scene despite our father's legendary affiliation, but we didn't knock what other people did. This generation's gangs were different from what my pop grew up doing. I mean, you never heard about the BGF in the news like bloods, crips, and all those million Spanish gangs on the street. My dad and his crew moved in silence and I could respect that. But it sounded like this nigga Monster wanted to make a little noise.

"Tell me what you know about Monster," I said.

"I don't know him, I swear. It was business," he declared, openly sobbing now.

For once, I actually believed him because I knew it had always been just business with Sandman, and because at that point, I thought he'd lie to God before me.

"I know it was just business, but they picked the wrong city to conduct business in. Big Baby, tighten him all the way up for me."

I knew grown men that would've turned away from what I was seeing, but my father had taught us to never take a life if we couldn't stomach how it ended. Tighter and tighter the vice ground into his skull until suddenly there was a loud crunch that echoed off the walls, and the screaming stopped.

"I thought he would never shut up. Throw him in the trunk of one of these cars and put a match to the whole building. I'll meet you out front," I said, pulling my phone back out as I headed for the side door.

I'd gotten pieces of the information we needed, but I didn't like the feeling of where this might be going. I waited until I was behind the wheel of my two thousand fifteen Mercedes-Benz G550 truck before I called Freedom, knowing she wasn't gonna like the news.

"What's up?" she asked on the third ring.

"It ain't good. Where you at?"

"I'm at the house on Grand Street right now," she replied.

"I'll be there in fifteen minutes."

"I'll wait," she said, disconnecting our call.

If this shit was what I thought it was then the good luck we'd thought we had just went out the window. From the day my father got locked up, we'd all had one mission and one goal in mind, and that was to make it to the top by any means. He who has the money has the power, and he who has the power makes the rules. Knowing that valuable lesson had made our mission clear and we'd spread out into different hustles so we could corner the market. We were schooled by the best in the game, the man who taught us that you couldn't win at monopoly just because you had Boardwalk and Park Place.

When you had the three yellow properties right before the 'go to jail' square and the three green after it, only then did you have the game sewed up. Why? Because everybody was worried about ducking jail, and they'd give up money to avoid it. For ten years, we'd been in the trenches collecting, and just when we thought we had the game won, here came some unexpected shit. One thing was for damn sure though, we'd come too far to go back, so whoever or whatever the situation was they better be ready to die 'bout theirs because we were bringing hell 'bout ours. I could smell the smoke moments before Big Baby came out the side door so I started my truck.

"Everything good?" I asked once he was sitting beside me with the door closed.

He nodded his head yeah and I put the warehouse in my rear-view mirror. It was crazy to me how everything was happening right then, at the exact moment when we needed to be keeping our heads down and our minds focused. The window to break dad out was so small and shit had to be precise because taking down a federal transport team wouldn't be easy. We decided on a team of six, which included us three and three more mufuckas we knew would bring that hammer when the time came. No one was trying to die, and we damn sure weren't going for getting captured, so we needed a clear head to execute the plan.

All this extra shit was a dangerous distraction. I pulled up in front of one of Free's trap houses to find her sitting out front waiting for me.

"Stay here, I'll be right back," I said, hopping out and going to her.

The sun was going down and the air had taken on a slight chill, but Free was sitting on the concrete steps in the same t-shirt and jeans she'd had on earlier. I had at least thrown a hoody on.

"What's up, sis?" I said, sitting next to her.

"Tired, and not looking forward to whatever it is you're about to say."

"I ain't gonna beat around the bush then. Word is that somebody specifically went after Deuce."

"I would ask, but ain't no telling what that nigga done did now. He's as trigger happy as he is horny. Who's trying to hit him?" she asked, sighing.

"Some nigga named Monster. He's supposed to be Hoover from Nashville."

"A Hoover? Then why the fuck would he be going after King Deuce?" she asked, looking at me.

"I don't know." I could see in her eyes that she was putting the pieces of the puzzle together as quickly as I was.

"Are you telling me we're somehow in the middle of a war, literally?" she asked.

"That's what it looks like. I don't know what's going on, but it's obvious the nigga tried to kill Deuce when he was out of town handling business to keep suspicion off himself. We won't know the full story until we talk to deuce. But there's something else we got to think about, too."

"What's that?"

"It's only going to be a certain amount of time before word gets back to this nigga, Monster, that the hitters he sent got slumped, and by who. You know what's next," I said.

"Yeah. We're going to end up slaying Monster."

Chapter Nine
Freedom

It was after 1:00 a.m. by the time we all got back under the same roof, and due to the long day she'd had, I insisted we meet at Angel's house. I'd been analyzing the situation in my head and I'd come to the conclusion that whatever the situation was we couldn't be involved until after our primary goal was accomplished. My father still hadn't greenlighted the prison break, but we'd done what he asked and taken care of Angel's situation. Technically, it wasn't over because she still had to go to court and face two charges of voluntary manslaughter, and hope the judge accepted the plea deal.

She was looking at a twenty-year suspended sentence with supervised probation for ten years, but it beat spending time in prison. I tried not to let my guilt show and simply express how grateful I was, but deep down I knew she wouldn't have been in the situation had it not been for me. It didn't matter that whoever had been after Deuce, because he wouldn't have been down here if it hadn't been for my dope. I felt like I'd failed Angel, but that was the last time I let that shit happen. I fully intended to address whatever the situation would be with this nigga Monster when the time came, but that could only be after my father was home.

First, I just needed to understand what Deuce had dragged us all into, which was why this late-night meeting of the minds was taking place. Looking around the glass dining room table, I could see how tired everybody was, but we couldn't walk around wanted by ignorance or we could end up dead.

"Here is the situation. While you two were at the police station, Destiny was gathering info on why a nigga tried to jack you and-"

"It was just some lil niggas trying to come up on a nice ride. I had my homies look into it," Deuce said.

"Yeah, well some of your homies ain't your homies, my nigga, because that shit wasn't random," Destiny replied.

"Fuck you talkin' 'bout?"

"What she's talking about is the nigga named Monster from Nashville orchestrated the whole thing," I said. The look on his face alone said he knew the name, which meant he knew what their beef was.

"Who is this nigga and what's the issue because, from what Destiny found out, this mufucka is Hoover, too," I said.

"Yeah, he is. He's five-deuce Hoover just like me. This shit is stupid, though, because me and him were beefin' when we were locked up in Tennessee, and it was for some dumb shit."

"Apparently, he still feels some type of way about it. So why don't you tell us what happened?" Destiny suggested.

"Basically, he was a big homie and I ended up at the same prison as him, and when you do that, you supposed to fall in line. I ain't got no problem with that, but I am a man before I'm anything else and a mufucka gonna respect that. Niggas already didn't like me because I'm from Memphis so any little issue was blown out of proportion. Shit got real and me and Monster had to handle our shit one on one like men."

"So, all of this is behind some penitentiary fight?" I asked.

"That and a bunch of he said she said, but at the end of the day, the nigga just wanted me to be scared of him and I ain't."

"Check this out my nigga, you know we all fuck with you like you family, but we got too much going on to get sucked into this drama right now. We rock with you and will ride for you, but we gotta handle the situation with our dad first," I said.

"And you know I respect that, but you ain't even gotta worry about that. Now that I know what it is, I'ma handle it. You hear me?"

"I hear you, bruh. Just try not to get yourself shot again," I replied sincerely.

"I won't, trust me."

"So, the niggas I shot, were they Hoover, too?" Angel asked.

"More than likely," Destiny replied.

"Don't even worry about that. I'ma handle it," Deuce said confidently.

I wasn't quite sure what he had in mind, but then again, I really didn't want to know. If he said he was going to handle it, then I believed him. That didn't mean I wasn't going to be ready for whatever whenever, because if a nigga came for me or mine, I was gonna put his whole family in boxes.

"Angel, you still gonna let me borrow your car?" Deuce asked her. Without hesitation, she reached in her pocket, pulled the key out, and slid it to him.

"Take the key to my truck, and when the cops release it, you can drive that until I get back. Before you say anything, I know it has to be fixed and cleaned, so here," he said, passing her the key and counting out ten one hundred dollar bills with it.

"What are you gonna do?" I asked.

"I'ma do what my man Kevin Hart said, I'ma peel his motherfuckin' muffin cap back." And with that, he headed for the door, disappearing into the night.

"That nigga crazy," Angel said, laughing.

"And that ain't no lie," Destiny said, shaking her head.

"How you holding up, Angel?" I asked on a serious note.

"Could be better, could be worse. I'm glad I ain't gotta do a bid, but I feel like I gotta walk on eggshells for the next decade."

"Whatever happens, you've got me and Destiny behind you," I assured her.

"And dad too, as soon as we can get him home. Speaking of which, maybe Angel should sit this one out," Destiny said slowly.

"Bitch, what? Don't try to play me like I can't handle business, Destiny. because that's gonna piss me off. This is my father we're talking about."

"He's all of our father, and I'm not saying you can't handle business, I'm simply expressing concern because you ain't even put no ink on the deal yet. If shit goes wrong, that plea agreement will vanish."

"Well then shit better not go wrong," Angel replied stubbornly.

I understood the logical side of Destiny's argument. I knew she was only giving voice to the truth we needed to pay attention to. At the same time, we all knew that we were in this together even if we had to operate with the mentality that the law couldn't touch us.

"We need to be as prepared as we can for this," I said, looking from one of them to the other.

"Destiny, what's our firepower look like? And, Angel, have they put the time or destination of the transfer on any official paperwork yet?"

"The guns are straight, we've got two AK-47's, an Uzi, two AR-15's and of course my Mossberg. All clean," Destiny replied first.

"And no they haven't put out anything new on dad," Angel said.

I didn't like how close to the chest they were playing our dad's transfer. The way it was looking, we'd be all dressed the fuck up with nowhere to go, and that didn't make for effective planning. What was the alternative, though?

"Did you call dad and let him know what happened with everything?" I asked Angel.

"I sent him a text, but he hasn't got back to me yet."

"You know he technically hasn't agreed to what we want to pull off," Destiny reminded me.

"I'm aware of that, but it don't matter because I'm not letting him die in there."

I watched the both of them exchange looks, but neither of them said anything because they felt the same as I did. It didn't matter what the courts thought he deserved, he was our father and this was our family. Fuck outside opinions.

"Did you get everything straight with the transportation after I left?" Angel asked.

"I got an old brinks truck to do the ram job and two dodge chargers for the getaway. I'ma drive one car and Bone is gonna drive the other. Is Big Baby good with running the truck into whatever the cops are driving?" I asked.

"You know that nigga is cray-cray and down for whatever, and he already hollered at his brother to move with us," Destiny replied.

Big Baby's brother was bigger than him, standing at six feet seven inches and weighing three hundred and twenty pounds, but the hood called him Lil Boy. I never understood that, but the nigga was bout that action and that was exactly what we needed for this job,

"Good. We're gonna run this like a simple smash and grab job. So as soon as Big Baby hits that transport, we hop out guns blazin'," I said.

"Guns blazin'? Won't they come at us harder if we kill cops, feds at that?" Angel asked.

"Yeah, but the only good witness is a dead one. Think about it, cops are trained to notice and remember the slightest details in a matter of moments, and the last thing we need is them noticing some insignificant shit we didn't consider that leads them to us. I'd rather kill'em than take that risk," I replied.

I could see the indecision on Angel's face, but she knew I was telling the truth. We'd seen countless TV shows where crooks got caught because their everyday behavior that they were unaware of caught a cop's attention, and the next thing you knew, they were getting their doors knocked down while they were sitting on the couch scratching their ass. Nah, not us, so if my sisters knew what was good for them, they'd send them cops home with a twenty-one-gun salute.

"What about the escape route," Destiny asked.

"Already got the private jet running for the twenty-first, destination to be given once he is on board."

"Where we going?" Angel asked.

"We ain't going nowhere just yet. We gotta act normal like we know nothing. These aren't local cops we killing, remember, so they're gonna be watching our ass closer than the Taliban. Dad will go to Brazil, where he can lay low without fear of extradition and, hopefully, in a year we can join him."

"A year?" they both exclaimed in unison.

"Are you two really not understanding how serious this shit is?" I asked with rising irritation.

"This ain't some made for TV movie shit we about to pull off. Going up against the biggest, most corrupt gang this world has ever seen, the government. This shit is gonna be on every news channel, talked about in every barbershop and hair salon across the country. Bitch, they're gonna hunt for the mufuckas behind this. So if it takes a year, five years, or ten years before we can relocate safely, then we'll have to wait. Is dad worth that?"

I didn't like the idea of waiting any more than they did, but we had to be way more than smart about this shit. We were talking life and death, nothing less. It would be crazy to go through with everything only to have it blow up in our faces because we were impatient.

"You're right, Free," Angel said.

"Tell us the rest of the plan."

"Well I figured ten million dollars would be enough to get him settled to where he ain't gotta poke his head out of hiding for a while. Destiny, you and I are gonna have to be squeaky clean for a while because if they can catch us doing anything they're gonna squeeze."

"True. I got enough paper put away to do something legit though, maybe put it together with Angel and open our own club," Destiny said, looking to Angel for her opinion.

"That could work. What about you, though, Free? You've built a quiet empire in these streets and it makes the most money out of all of us," Angel said.

"You're right, and it's gonna keep making money. Bone and I already sat down about him running the day to day while I play the background, so it's all good."

"You trust him with a damn near one hundred million dollar a year business?" Destiny asked.

"I don't trust no one, except you bitches, but Bone knows one universal truth. You never make an enemy out of someone who knows your deepest fears," I replied confidently.

"Preach," Angel said, smiling.

Looking at my phone, I saw that it was almost two a.m., which meant I needed to get my ass home and finally get some sleep.

"We can talk more tomorrow," I said, standing up and stretching.

"When are you gonna fill dad in?" Destiny asked.

"There's no need for him to know how we're coming so I'll tell him as much as he needs to know tomorrow."

"Cool. I'ma stay the night here since the virgin Angel ain't got a car," Destiny said.

"Aww, that's mighty white of you," Angel replied, sticking her tongue out.

After giving both of them a hug, I made my way downstairs and hopped on my bike, making the drive to my quiet suburban neighborhood in fifteen minutes. Typically, it wasn't a smart move for a dope dealer to have a big house, but after spending years in the gutter and smelling the piss in the hallway on the regular, I needed something to give me a peace of mind. I hadn't gotten outrageous, though, because it was only a four bedroom, two and a half bathroom, one level house with a garage and a fenced-in back yard.

I didn't want a mansion, I'd just wanted something that was my own. Pulling into the garage, I parked alongside the silver 2011 Porsche 911 GT3, making sure to hit the button to close the garage on my way into the house. After disarming and rearming the alarm system, I went through the kitchen and dining room straight into the living room, where I collapsed on the couch. My body was pleading with me not to move and I damn sure wasn't in the mood to argue with myself. Within moments, I found the sanctuary of sleep, and I stayed there until I felt myself being lifted as if I weighed no more than a feather.

"Baby," I mumbled.

"Shh, I got you. Just go back to sleep," he replied, carrying me.

The next thing I knew, he was laying me down on our bed and undressing me from the waist down. I knew he wasn't doing that to entice sex out of me, but to be real, I needed my man as much as I needed sleep. Once he had my socks, shoes, and pants off, he made as if to lay down beside me, but I pulled him on top of me instead.

"Baby, you need to get some sleep. You've been running non-stop."

"I know, but I missed you," I replied, running my hand down the smooth hardness of his chest until I reached his shorts.

"I'll be here when you wake up," he assured me, but I could tell by the change in his breathing that he wanted what I did.

"Bone, stop talking and fuck me," I demanded, reaching in his shorts and grabbing ahold of his throbbing dick.

He had no room left to protest once I opened my legs because I didn't have any panties on. But he was beyond fighting his needs, and he pushed inside me hard enough to take my breath away.

"Take what y-you want," I told him, locking my legs behind his back to ensure that I felt his presence in my stomach.

His kisses conveyed his hunger and he punctuated their passion with devastating blows that made my toes curl.

"Bone," I screamed when he put my legs on his shoulders and started feeding me strokes that had my eyes rolling.

I hadn't even came yet, but I could feel my pussy juices running down the crack of my ass. The storm was real and the struggle to hold on was becoming more real with each pounding blow.

"Baby, baby, I-I'm gonna cum," I warned.

His response was to push on my legs until I was damn near folded in half, while drilling me harder with that good dick. In an instant, lightening exploded in our bedroom and the flood gates opened as we came together. It was always that intense and I could never stop the shaking in my legs that came with that experience.

"I-I needed that," I panted, searching for air to fill my lungs.

"M-Me too," he sighed rolling off me and onto his side of the bed.

No one really knew about this part of our relationship, and the dick was so good I had to keep it a secret. The streets might perceive this as a weakness, and neither of us could afford that. As our heart rates began to slow, he pulled me closer to him and I knew I'd wake up in the same embrace we often slept in. That put a smile on my face because he was a gangsta in the street, but a teddy bear inside these four walls. I'd just found the land of peaceful dreams when the sound of my phone snatched me back.

"Is that yours?" he asked.

"Yeah," I moaned, already dreading getting out of bed.

Nobody called this late unless it was trouble. Being the good dude he was, Bone got up and got my phone out of my jeans pocket, and one look at the number calling spelled all types of bad news.

"What is it, Destiny?" I asked.

"It's dad. He didn't answer his phone, someone else did."

"Who?" I asked, coming fully awake.

"It was a CO. I don't know what happened, but dad got caught up somehow."

Chapter Ten
Destiny

The battle between me and sleep was one for the record books. I knew I needed to sleep, but not knowing what was going on with my father had fear prying my eyelids open. I tried listening to Free when she told me that there was nothing we could do in the middle of the night except sleep, but it still took hours before I drifted back off. Normally, I didn't have a problem getting comfortable on Angel's couch, but I was beyond restless and somewhat relieved when I opened my eyes to find the room bathed in morning sunlight.

I was still tired as fuck, but at least now I could get something done. My first phone call was to the prison to find out what my father's status was because getting caught with a cellphone meant time in the box. It wouldn't be his first time in the no way out, it was just the wrong time for this shit to happen. The phone must've rang thirty times and still no one picked up. I hung up and tried again, getting the same results, which had me tempted to break my mufuckin' phone.

"Did you sleep?" Angel asked, going into the kitchen and getting some orange juice.

"If you could call it that. I hate not knowing what's going on with dad, that shit has gotten me feeling all kinds of antsy."

"I mean, sometimes shit happens. You know pops can handle his own and do whatever time they give him in the hole," she replied.

"It ain't about that. Now is not the time for this, and I want to know how he got caught up in the first place."

"What did they say when you called?" she asked, pouring me a glass of orange juice and bringing it to me.

"Mufuckas ain't answering, goddamn phone just keeps ringing."

“So why not call that bitch you fucked and find out what the business is,” she suggested.

After taking a drink of juice, I scrolled through my phone until I came to Kimberlee’s number. But when I hit send, it didn’t ring. I hung up and tried again. That time I got a message saying that the number was no longer in service.

“What’s wrong? Why you got that look on your face?” Angel asked.

“Her number is disconnected.”

“When was the last time you talked to her?”

“When I was threatening her mufuckin’ ass,” I replied, not liking the feeling I was getting.

“You know what dad would say, there’s no such thing as coincidences.”

The truth in that statement didn’t make me feel any better. In fact, it only intensified the feeling of doom I had. I tried calling the prison again, but I still didn’t get an answer, so I sent Freedom a text, letting her know about this latest development. I didn’t know what was going on, but I didn’t feel like I could accomplish shit being so far away.

“Maybe she changed her number because she never wants to hear from you. Maybe you just scared her that bad,” Angel pointed out.

“Yeah, maybe,” I said, already on the jet blue airlines website checking ticket prices and departure times for flights into Baltimore-Washington international airport.

I was determined to get answers and I knew I wasn’t ‘bout to get them sitting on Angel’s couch. Part of me wanted to wait until Free got back at me before I made any moves, but at the same time she’d always told us to trust our instincts. I quickly bought a one-way ticket for a flight leaving in two hours and made sure to rent a car that was fast.

"I ain't got time to go to my apartment so I'm barrowing some of your clothes," I informed her, heading in the direction of her bedroom.

"Why don't you got time, what are you about to do?" she asked, hot on my heels.

"I'ma find out what the fuck is going on because I've got a bad feeling. And if this does have something to do with that bitch, then I'm gonna fix it."

"Wait, so you're going back up there now?"

"Yep," I replied, going into her bathroom and starting the shower.

"Are you sure that's the smartest move? I mean, you could be taking a trip all the way up there for nothing."

"What else can I do, Angel? We have no idea what's going on behind those walls up there, and the only mufucka who can provide answers ain't answering her damn phone. I know that bitch will answer her door, though," I said, stripping out of my jeans and t-shirt before I stepped into the water spray.

"Maybe she ain't the only one who can get answers," I heard Angel say before she walked out of the bathroom.

Knowing her, she was probably getting ready to call Free. But either way, my mind was made up about going back to Baltimore. We all had to be up there in a few days to handle business, so I was just getting a head start. I took a fast shower, but I still felt completely refreshed when I got out and went to Angel's closet to find something to wear. We definitely didn't have the same fashion sense, but I found a white velour sweat suit and grabbed a Muhammad Ali t-shirt to go with it. I was in a rush, which meant no bra and panties required. Within five minutes, I was dressed with my braids tucked under a fitted cap.

"Did you pick your clothes up off my floor?" Angel asked when I walked back into the living room.

"Yeah, bitch, they're in your dirty clothes hamper."

"I gotta ask because you don't like to pick up after yourself."

"Whatever. Did you call Free?" I asked, slipping my feet into my Jordan's and checking my phone to see if she'd responded to my text message.

"No, not yet, but I did call that lawyer, Miranda Sorenson. I figured that if a prison official had to answer to anybody, it would be a lawyer, especially if they don't want a big ass lawsuit."

"Good move," I replied, sending Free another text to tell her I was headed back North. I made sure to let Big Baby know, too, just in case he came looking for me.

"When are you coming to Baltimore?" I asked.

"Probably tomorrow or the day after, I'm gonna work tonight just to put some more money in my pocket."

"You got the car you're gonna make the drive in?"

"I think me and Free are coming up in her Porsche, but I don't know because riding with that much fire power in a car that sticks out might not be smart," she replied

"Looking at it from a different perspective how many cop cars do you think can catch that Porsche because you know she ain't 'bout to pull over," I commented.

"True."

"Well listen, if that lawyer finds anything out, let me know, and if I find something out, I'll message you and Free," I said, heading for the door.

"Be safe, love you."

"Love you, too," I replied, closing the door and dialing Free's number.

I really wanted to talk with her before I left, not because I needed permission, but because I would feel better knowing we were all on the same page. I wanted her to tell me that I was worried about nothing, but as I heard her voicemail come on, I knew I wouldn't get that comfort right now. I hung up, hopped in my truck, and headed to the nearest McDonald's to grab breakfast since I still had time to kill.

I was halfway through my sausage, egg, and cheese biscuit when I got the feeling of being watched. I didn't panic or switch up my movements in the slightest, I just became more aware of my surroundings. So far, there was no one that stuck out as a threat or as someone who didn't belong, but I was too seasoned in the street life to dismiss what I was feeling. I was being watched. It only took me a couple of minutes to finish my meal and get back to my truck. The first thing I did once I was inside was reach in the middle console for the comforting grip of my Glock .19.

There was no need to check the clip or the chamber because I knew that bitch was ready to bark, and it was legal, so if shit got real, I'd be okay. I tucked the pistol under my right leg before starting my truck and pulling off into traffic. I made sure my eyes hit every mirror in ten to fifteen second rotations, but I still wasn't spotting whatever or whoever had my senses on high alert. Most street niggas weren't professional in the art of surveillance without being spotted, so either I was trippin, it was a professional hunter, or it was the law.

I ruled one out immediately and kept my eyes peeled behind my tinted windows. My ringing phone was a distraction I didn't need at the moment. When I got it out and saw who it was, I had to answer.

"Where you at?"

"I'm at home. I just got up. Where the hell are you?" Free asked.

"I'm on my way to the airport, but I'm taking a detour first."

"A detour? Why?"

"Because somebody's watching me or following me," I replied, switching lanes quickly.

"Hold up, one thing at a time. Do you really think you need to go all the way to Baltimore just because dad got caught with a phone?"

"We don't know what dad got caught with or how, but I wanted answers and I don't like the fact that the bitch Kimberlee changed her number."

"What do you think that's about?" Free asked.

"I don't know. All I know is that the whole situation don't feel very good to me, so I'm going to find out what's shakin'."

"Okay. What makes you think you're being followed?"

"Just a feeling," I replied, making a sudden right turn.

"Keep your eyes open and be safe. Call me when you know something, and I'll do the same."

"A'ight, love you."

"Love you too," she replied, hanging up.

I still hadn't caught sight of whoever was out there, but the apprehensive feelings I had weren't subsiding in the slightest. I moved through the city as normal as counter surveillance would allow, waiting until the last minute to head for the airport. I didn't wanna part with my gun, but there was no way around it, so I locked it in my glove compartment and made a mad dash into the terminal. Sleep deprivation had me on edge already, so when I factored in the feeling of me being watched and having to surround myself with a sea of strangers, I could understand my nerves being shot.

Still, I maintained my composure and managed to board my flight without issue. I didn't take my first deep breath until we were thirty thousand feet and climbing, but after two shots of Cîroc, I was able to doze off for a needed nap. Thankfully, the worry for my father and the unease of being watched didn't follow me into my sleep, and by the time I woke up, I had a clear-headed path of action. I sent Angel a text to see if she'd heard anything from the lawyer, but she said it might take a few hours. That gave me enough time to pay sweet Kimberlee a visit.

Once the plane landed, I went to the rental car place and got the keys to my 2015 Lamborghini Huracan, itching to get behind the wheel. A lambo didn't exactly blend in, but it gave me the speed I wanted to get where I had to go. After I got dropped off at the car, I pulled up Kimberlee's address, put it in the GPS, and I was gone. It wasn't until I was sitting in front of her building that I realized I'd made the trip without any type of weapon on me. For the first time today, I smiled, because my hands were as nice as my trigger play.

I parked a couple of buildings away from hers and walked back, checking my surroundings to see who might've been watching me. Taking the stairs two at a time, I got to her floor and I was just about to kick her door in when it swung open. Her eyes got as wide as the rims on my rental and they were drowning in a fear that left her paralyzed for five seconds too long. My opening statement was a swift right left combination that stumbled her back into the apartment, and I advanced quickly, shutting the door behind me.

"Miss me?" I asked, firing a hook that put her on her ass.

"What, what the fuck," she said, holding her hands up in surrender.

"Bitch, don't act like you don't know why I'm here," I said, standing over her, acting as if I knew more than I did.

"It-it wasn't my fault. Someone snitched on both of us, and I got fired."

"Lie to me if you want to, bitch, and your son will watch you die," I promised.

"I ain't lying, I swear."

I stood there for a moment and contemplated what she was saying, knowing how high the probability of truth was. Niggas in prison told on small things so big shit was definitely fair game. My thought process was interrupted by my phone ringing, and I pulled it out and answered without looking at it.

"Yeah?"

"He's gone! Destiny, he's gone!"

"Who?" I asked.

"Dad!"

Chapter Eleven
Angel

"Destiny! Did you hear what the fuck I said?" I yelled, fighting the hysteria rising within me.

"Slow down and explain what happened, Angel," she said.

I had to take two deep breaths before I was composed enough to speak again. "I talked to the lawyer and she said that dad was transferred in the middle of the night, no warning or nothing."

"Transferred? That's gotta be bullshit because we know his transfer was scheduled for the twenty-first," she replied.

"That's what I said, but Miranda said that's the story she got from the warden of the prison, and dad is no longer in that database."

"So, where the fuck is he?"

"That's the part that has me panicked because Miranda said the prison claims they don't know where he was moved to. And I can't find him anywhere in the federal database using his name and inmate number," I said with growing fear.

"Wait, are you trying to tell me dad just vanished? You know that shit ain't possible."

"So where is he then?" I asked.

Silence came in the place I'd hoped to find a reassuring answer, but I wasn't surprised because no logical answer seemed to fit.

"What did Free say?" she finally asked.

"She's looking into it. Find out what that bitch knows."

"I'll call you back," she said, hanging up before I could say another word. I was just about to call Free when I heard my front door opening, which meant she was here.

"What'd you find out?" I asked, coming up the hallway and meeting her in the kitchen.

"I can't get the warden of the prison on the phone, and sources say the transportation advisor position hasn't been filled yet, so I have no idea who's making those decisions."

"So, what are we gonna do?"

"Pack a bag really quick because we're going to B-More A.S.A.P," she replied.

I didn't need to be told twice, I immediately went to my room and started throwing shit into a duffel bag. I made sure all the clothing was black and I packed enough for me and Destiny since she only had the clothes on her back. Within ten minutes, I was ready to move.

"What time is our flight?" I asked, coming back into the kitchen.

"We're driving and my car's out front, so let's go."

After making sure my spot was locked up tight, we headed for the parking lot. As soon as we got out front, I knew Free was taking this seriously because parked right behind her Porsche was Bone's white 2014 Porsche Cayenne GTS with him at the wheel, and Big Baby and Lil' Boy occupying the front and back seats. I put my bag in the trunk and hopped in Free's passenger seat.

"How long will it take us to get there?" I asked.

"I don't know. We're gonna really find out what this car can do," she replied, smoking the tires as we pulled out of the parking lot.

"So what's the play when we get there?"

"Have you talked to Destiny yet?" she asked.

"Just before you got to my house."

"We're gonna link up with her as soon as we get there and then we're gonna pay the warden a visit. Text Destiny and let her know we're on the way," she said, merging onto the highway and snatching gears like a race car driver.

At first I was worried that Bone wouldn't be able to keep up, but every time I glanced in the side mirror, he was right behind us.

When I'd put my bag in the trunk, I'd seen the assortment of weapons we were moving with, and I knew there were plenty more in the trunk behind us. My hope was that the radar detector Free had installed worked like it was supposed to.

"What do you think is going on, Free?"

"I don't know, it could be a few things. Maybe they thought he was trying to break himself out after he got caught with the phone and they factored in the transportation advisor's family being murdered. Maybe they just moved the transfer date up to keep dad always guessing, or maybe he was the only transfer for a while so they got it done early. I honestly don't know what's going on, but I promise you that we're gonna find out. Then we're gonna find dad and put an end to this shit."

She spoke with the same determination that she'd had my whole life. That iron will she had and her refusal to bend or compromise is how we'd survived without our parents' guidance. The streets are anything but merciful, especially for young women because niggas wanted to fuck us and then fuck us over. Freedom had her education and degree in ruthless, though, and she'd taught us because failure wasn't an option then, any more than it is now.

"Destiny just texted back and said she's interrogating, but she'll call when she's done."

"Knowing her and how much she enjoys her work, we might be in Baltimore before she's done," Free replied, swerving in and out of lanes.

"If that sneaky bitch knows anything, I want parts of her, too," I said, sending Destiny a text telling her the exact same thing.

"Here, take this," she said, handing me her phone.

"Find Black Sam's number and find out if there's anything new."

Black Sam was our homegirl Samantha who'd been our go to when it came to matters that refigured technical support. She didn't look like she knew her way through cyberspace, but that bitch was a whiz with the keyboard, and if there was anyone who could find our father, it would be her. I shot her a text and waited, hating the fact that I was forced to be patient about something this serious. I never denied missing my mother because in truth I did, but as I got older, I came to terms with what happened and why it happened.

Something about this whole situation made me feel like I was losing my father now, and there was no way I could ever deal with that. No matter what went down or what we had to do, we were bringing him home.

"Black Sam said she's still looking," I said, reading her text aloud.

"She'll find him."

I had the same faith in her because to believe anything different might cause me to doubt our mission as a whole. I continued checking in with her and other contacts Free had until I fell asleep somehow. When I woke up, the moon had replaced the sun and it was high in the sky, but there were still plenty of cars on the road with us.

"W-what time is it and where are we?" I asked.

"It's a little after one a.m. and we're in B-More."

"You got us here in ten hours? Damn, you were pushing," I said, stretching as much as I could given the confines of the car.

"I'm motivated," she replied simply. A quick look in the side mirror revealed that Bone had kept pace with us the whole way.

"Where are we going?"

"To meet up with Destiny at the Super Eight Motel and put our plan together. I'm not trying to waste no time," she replied.

Her words echoed my sentiments exactly, and whatever we had to do to get the answers we needed would be done. It took us another twenty minutes before we pulled up in the parking lot.

"Grab both bags," Free said, getting out of the car, meaning my clothes and hers.

"We got rooms one-hundred and six, one-hundred and seven, and one-hundred and eight. Big Baby and Lil Boy take room one-hundred and six, Bone you're in room one-hundred and eight, and we're in room one-hundred and seven. Hold up while I get the keys," Free said, disappearing into the office.

I grabbed our bags and headed for our room, kicking the door so Destiny would open it.

"Damn, you all made it up here quick," she said, stepping aside to let me in.

"She put wings on the side of that bad mufucka, I'm telling you. How you holding up?" I asked.

"Maintaining, what about you?"

"Just ready to get some answers," I replied, throwing my bag of clothes on one of the two beds and taking the bag of guns to the little table sitting by the window.

The room was basic, two beds, table, T.V., and a bathroom, but it was clean and would serve its purpose.

"I want answers, too, but you all need to get some sleep before we make this next move," she advised.

"I slept in the car, but you can try to talk Free into it and see how far that gets you."

"Talk me into what?" Free asked, coming through the door, followed by Bone, Big Baby, and Lil Boy.

"Getting some sleep," Destiny replied. The look Freedom gave her said it all, so we moved on.

"A'ight we all know what the situation is and why we're here. What have you found out so far?" Free asked, looking at Destiny.

"The CO bitch ain't know nothing, for real. She said someone obviously seen her give dad the phone because not a good two days later he gets caught with it and she got fired."

"Do you believe her?" I asked.

"She was very convincing and in no position to lie," Destiny replied, smiling.

We all knew what that smile meant so there was no need to ask if Kimberlee would call the police. A dead man or woman tells no tales.

"I did get the wardens home address," Destiny added.

"Yeah, Black Sam verified that it was the right one and it's about an hour from here, in Fredrick, Maryland. When do you wanna go?" I asked.

"Now," Free replied, digging in the duffel bag on the table and pulling out her beloved Mossberg.

"You do need to sleep, Free. We both just pushed a ten hour drive," Bone said.

He'd known Free a long time, which meant he should've been able to read the warning signs before he got cussed out, and a big one had been the look she'd given when Destiny suggested the same thing. She turned to say something to Bone, but I caught her eye before she could open her mouth, and I shook my head. I saw her visibly calm herself and take a deep breath. I looked at Bone, knowing that he had no idea I'd just saved his life.

"I'm not tired, and that needs to be the last time anyone suggests sleep to me. I'll sleep when I'm ready," Free informed us all, making sure to make eye contact with each person in the room. Nobody said a word and it was probably a wise decision.

"Let's go," Free said, heading for the door. Destiny and I grabbed AR-15's out of the bag and followed her.

"Angel, you ride with Destiny. Big Baby and Lil Boy take my truck," Bone said, tossing them his keys before he climbed into the passenger seat of Free's car.

I looked at Destiny and saw she was looking at me, but I shook my head because if Bone wanted to verbally get his head blown back then that was his decision.

"Leave it to you to rent a damn Lambo," I said, going to the passenger side of the car.

"Yeah, but at least I got it in dark blue instead of the candy apple red they first offered me," Destiny said, laughing.

Bitch don't know how to blend in for nothing, I thought, shaking my head. Once everybody was loaded up, we took our show on the road, moving through the shadows at a high rate of speed with one mission, finding our father. We made the hour drive in forty-five minutes flat, creeping into the sleepy middle class neighborhood like thieves in the night. We all stopped on the street behind the house we wanted. then we got out with our guns ready and circled back around. The thing about moving with a team of people that we were familiar with was that we didn't have to speak on how shit needed to go.

The men took the back and we took the front, me on the front door with Free and Destiny watching my back. I'd already gotten the security code from Black Sam, but now I need some luck in the form of a cheap lock. With a top notch security system, a lot of people felt a dead bolt was excessive and unnecessary, at least those in white America who'd never had their door knocked down. We knew warden Scott Diggs was in the house with his wife, Millie, and their teenage son, William, and now it was time to give them a rude awakening.

"Y'all ready?" I whispered, turning around to look at my sisters.

Both women nodded their heads. I took a quick breath and then planted my foot with all my weight behind it right next to the lock, loving the sound of splintering wood as the doorframe gave way. I wasted no time running to the alarm while Free went to open the back door, and Destiny bolted up the staircase that was directly inside and to the left. As soon as I had the alarm shut off, I closed the door and moved into the living room that was directly to the right.

The only light was what the moon was providing, but for now, that would do, and it would increase the fear factor. I took a seat on the couch and was soon joined by Free and Bone while Big Baby and Lil Boy went upstairs to help Destiny. For a second, I heard the beginnings of a scream, but it was cut off as quickly as it started. Within a matter of minutes, the Diggs family was joining us in their living room, but I could smell their fear long before we shared the same air.

"Mr. Diggs, we're in your home tonight because we want information, and the sooner you give us that information, the sooner all this will be over." Free said.

"I don't give a fuck why you're in my house. If you don't get the fuck out quick, you're all going to jail," he replied with false bravado.

"Ordinarily, I'd tell you not to try my patience, but I don't have any patience at the moment. Somebody turn the lights on," Free said, rising from the couch, cradling her shotgun. When the table light illuminated the room, I got the chance to see Free's eyes and I knew she'd gone from zero to a hundred.

"Lil Boy, bend him over the back of the couch and pull his pajamas down," Free ordered.

The warden tried to fight, but one punch from Lil Boy left a dazed look swimming in his eyes. Before he knew it, he was ass out and shaking. Free didn't say anything, she just walked up behind him and shoved the barrel of the Mossberg up his ass and chambered a shell. His screams were expected as were the tears of his family, but neither moved any of us whatsoever.

"Before I blow your colon through your throat, I'm gonna give you the chance to take back what you said because you obviously don't know that I'm not the bitch you wanna fuck with."

Chapter Twelve
Freedom

Scott Diggs was a medium height, overweight white man with a receding hair line and bad teeth. His son, William, resembled him a lot, right down to the bug-eyed look he was giving at the sight of my shotty invading his father's sphincter. The smile I gave William was genuine because the situation was funny, but even with the smile, I knew he didn't miss the look that told him it could be him.

"Are you gonna apologize, warden?" I asked politely.

"I'm sorry. I'm sorry," he screamed, trying to squirm away in vain.

"Good, now I want you to listen to me closely because we're in a hurry. Approximately twenty-four hours ago, Johnathan Walker was transferred from your prison without notice and I want to know why, and where he was moved to."

"I don't know, it wasn't my call. The U.S Marshalls took him!"

"Where did they take him?" I asked as calmly as I could.

"I don't know. Ask my wife."

At the mention of her, I turned my attention to the slim brunette, who was silently crying under Big Baby's watchful gaze. Her looks were average at best with her flat blue eyes, squared chin, and long nose, but she was still out of her husband's league.

"What do you know?" I asked.

"N-nothing I swear."

"Lil Boy, switch with Big Baby," I ordered, making sure my finger was on the trigger in case he so much as farted. Once Lil Boy had ahold on Millie, I gave her another chance.

"Millie, I'ma level with you woman to woman. There are things worse than death as your husband can bare witness to, but I don't wanna have to do those things to you. Just tell me what you know."

"I-I don't know anything," she insisted.

"Lil Boy," I said.

Instantly she was yanked off her feet by her throat in his iron grip, her legs swinging and searching for the safety of earth. Within ten seconds, her face was crimson in color, matching the veins in her eyes, but I still didn't signal him to lower her for ten additional seconds. This all was done just to get her attention.

"It only gets worse before it gets better," I warned.

"I-I don't know where he is," she said coughing mightily.

"So why did your husband suggest I ask you?"

"I don't know," she yelled.

"Warden," I said, pushing the shotgun up his ass harder and deeper.

He screamed right before his bowels loosened and he shit all over the place, I wanted to kill him, but I couldn't until I was sure I had all the information out of him.

"I'm waiting, warden," I said with a hand over my mouth, trying not the breath the funk in.

"She works for the bureau of prisons!"

"Shut the fuck up, Scott," his wife yelled at him.

"Lil Boy, give her some act right," I said.

As a woman, I knew a woman's fears, and I wasn't above exploiting that. There were no rules to the game anymore. There were only winners and losers, and it was my job to make sure my team won. Still holding her by her throat, Lil Boy grabbed a fistful of her flannel nightgown and ripped it off her body, leaving her wearing nothing except her cotton panties.

"Nice nipples," Destiny commented.

Lil Boy moved his grip from her throat to her hair and then he pulled his dick out, forcing her to look down at it. Now the whole family was wearing that same bug-eyed look, but I knew hers was because of what she knew was about to happen with what she was looking at. Lil Boy was swinging eight inches when it was soft, which meant he could do damage when that mufucka was rock hard. Knowing she was gonna be violated came with a certain fear of its own, but knowing she was gonna be fucked with that took the fear to a different level.

He wasted no time bending her over the couch right next to her husband, snatching her panties down, and plowing into her savagely. I thought her head might pop off with the first blow. But the scream got stuck in her throat because the second stroke was longer and harder.

"Hold up, bruh, let's see if she wants to talk now," I said.

"I don't know where he is," she insisted, crying almost hysterically.

I saw William flinch, but I didn't know if his brain was telegraphing a move he intended to make or he was tightening his ass cheeks up because he didn't wanna end up like his parents. The fear was etched in the pimples on his young face.

"Why was he moved ahead of schedule?" I asked.

"Because-because the warden thought he w-was plotting something."

"Warden?" I said turning my attention back to my own victim.

"Get it out of me please," he begged.

"You know, warden, since your wife is obviously more connected than you, I don't see why you should endure this anymore," I said sincerely.

When I pulled the trigger, I saw his whole back explode. But other than the Mossberg's roar, the room was completely silent. William's eyes had gone blank, and I knew whatever he was seeing wasn't in the room anymore. Millie had gone completely still, and the right side of her body was covered in the blood, guts, and waste of the man she'd once exchanged vows with.

"Millie? Millie, can you hear me?" I asked, moving around until I was directly in front of her.

Her head hung in a way that made her hair cover her eyes, but I stuck the shotgun under her chin and lifted it until we were making steady eye contact.

"Please don't kill me. I had nothing to do with Walker's transfer and I don't know where he is," she sobbed.

"But you know who has the answers we need," Angel said.

"Tracy Jordan. Tracy Jordan is who you want, not me. Please."

"Who is she?" Angel asked, already passing her gun to Destiny and pulling her phone out.

"She's my boss. She'll have all the answers you want. Now get him out of me."

"Big Baby," I said nodding towards a shaking William.

"Not my son," she yelled, trying to get loose from Lil Boy's grip.

"I'ma be real with you, Millie, neither of you are gonna live through this. But since you were helpful, and if the name you gave me is valid, then I'll give you a couple of options," I said.

"Black Sam said Tracy is the assistant director and she's getting all the information we need on her right now," Angel interjected.

"Well then, Millie, here's how it goes. You can watch your son die or you can die before him, and I'll even let you get a nut, since it'll be your last and I'm sure you've never had a dick that big," I told her.

"Please. Just let us go and we won't say anything. I promise," she begged.

"Millie," I said with more patience than I felt.

"I can't watch my son die. What mother can endure that?"

"Your last wish is granted. Big Baby, take him into another room. Destiny, I know what you wanna do, so take Angel with you. And Bone, find what we need to destroy all the evidence," I said, taking a step back and lowering my shotgun.

"Mom," William screamed before Big Baby cut off his air supply by putting him in a headlock and dragging him from the room.

Everybody else moved to take care of their specified task, leaving me, Millie, and Lil Boy in the living room alone.

"You're a monster," Millie screamed at me, crying harder.

"I know, but consider yourself lucky that I'm not gonna torture you. And I'm allowing you to die with a smile on your face."

"Fuck you, bitch," she said, her eyes alive and glowing with hate.

My response was to smile and nod at Lil Boy, who in turn got a fresh grip of her long hair and started pumping away. I estimated Millie's age as closer to fifty than forty, and even though she wasn't exactly ugly, I doubted she was going to the hood and turning niggas heads to get what she was getting now. I could tell when he dove deep inside her because her grunts matched the painful scrunching of her face. I'd always been curious about something I'd been told when I was growing up, about how white women often fantasized about Mandingo warriors taking the pussy.

While I could see everything in Millie telling her to fight, little by little, stroke by stroke, I witnessed her giving herself over to her darkest desires. Suddenly, her grunts had become more like moans and her tears weren't coming so frequently. When Lil Boy let her hair go and grabbed her by her waist, I could've sworn I saw her throw that ass back at him, but it wasn't until she closed her eyes that I know the truth. Every woman knew ecstasy when she saw it, and the fact that she could get there with what remained of her husband still dripping next to her said a lot. She may have thought I was evil, but there was something savage in all of us.

"She cum on that dick yet, bruh?" I asked.

"Twice," he grunted, fucking her faster. Her eyes sprang open at my question, shame showing brightly because she could no longer deny what her body was admitting.

"It's good, ain't it, Millie," I teased. I could see that flash of hate again, but it was wasted on me.

"Give her one more and be done with her," I said.

"I'm b-begging you pl-"

"Millie, you're wasting time talking to me. I suggest you enjoy your last ride," I advised her.

She opened her mouth as if to plead her case again, but I guess she saw the finality on my face and knew it was pointless. The next words she spoke were completely unexpected.

"Harder," she mumbled.

"What?" Lil Boy asked confused.

"H-harder," she growled through clenched teeth.

She'd obviously come to terms with this being the end because now she wasn't just getting fucked, she was fucking him back. That shit had Lil Boy trying to go crazy. Before I knew it, he'd pulled out, spent her around, and had her balanced on the back of the couch facing him. She kicked them panties off with a quickness so he could step between her legs and get back inside her, grabbing her by the throat so she'd be leaning back without falling. I watched in amazement as she wrapped her legs around his waist so she'd have the leverage to lift up into his powerful strokes.

"Yo, she's taking that dick," Destiny said in admiration, coming down the stairs carrying a jewelry box.

"Indeed," I replied.

This time when she came she let it be known by the sound of her strangled screams, and Lil Boy came with her. No sooner had her legs dropped from around his waist, he tightened the grip on her throat and twisted viciously, causing a loud snap to echo off the walls.

"Damn, you ain't even take the dick out of her, bruh. That's how you slay a bitch," Destiny said, laughing.

Lil Boy let her body drop next to her husband's remains just as Bone came back into the room.

"I found a fireplace in the kitchen and there's gas for the lawnmower on the deck by the back door so it's time to make our move."

"Angel," Destiny hollered.

"I'm right here," she replied, coming down the stairs with a backpack strapped to her back.

"Where's Big Baby?" I asked.

"He's putting the boy's body in the kitchen where the fire is gonna burn the hottest, and you should do the same thing," Bone said, looking at Lil Boy.

"We all go out the same way we came in. Angel, disarm the alarm and let's get out of here," I said.

Lil Boy picked up the late Millie Diggs and took her in the direction of the kitchen with Bone behind him, and we retraced our steps. Within five minutes, we were loaded back up and on the road back to the motel. I let Bone drive back, despite the argument we'd had on the way up there because I knew he'd only came at me about my lack of rest because he was concerned. The independent woman in me found it hard to let a man take care of me, especially since the only man who'd ever done it right was my father.

Still, I knew Bone was a good dude and I needed to cut him some slack. It was my intention to tell him just that, but it seemed like, as soon as I got comfortable in the passenger seat, sleep finally came for me and it wouldn't be denied. Sometimes, no matter how hard you fight to stay awake, your body shuts down because it has no other option. I awoke to the feeling of a hand lightly shaking me, but I didn't panic because I remembered where I was when I went to sleep.

"Guess I was tired, huh?" I said, smiling at Bone.

"You know I'm smart enough not to say I told you so, but I'm wondering where you intending to go back to sleep?"

"Wouldn't you like to know," I replied, opening the door and getting out of the car.

We all piled back into mine and my sisters' room to plan our next move.

"Black Sam sent Tracy's address. It's in Rockville, Maryland, which is a few hours from here," Angel said once everyone had found somewhere to sit.

"It's almost five a.m. We need to sleep before we make any more moves," Bone said, looking directly at me from his position on the bed across from me.

"Agreed," I said, fighting the smile that wanted to tilt my lips.

"I ain't tired," Angel said.

"Me either," Destiny chimed in.

"So why don't we ride out to this bitch's house and do some recon? She's married to some senator and they both got money, so it'd be good to get a look at the house before we popped up to do our thing," Angel said.

Destiny was already nodding her head like she was with it. But they both still looked my way to see what my response was.

"I'm cool with it. Just make sure you're careful and don't get caught," I warned.

"You want us to mob with you?" Lil Boy asked.

"Nah, you two need to get some rest, and Lil Boy, you need to wash your dick because I know that bitch bled on you. Besides, you niggas don't blend in well, and it sounds like they going to a white neighborhood," I replied, smiling. Big Baby shot a middle finger at me, which made us laugh.

"We can handle it," Destiny said.

"We'll check shit out and be back with a thorough report and a plan of attack."

"Make sure your phones are working and charged. And get something to eat while you're at it," I said.

"Yes, mother," Destiny replied sarcastically, causing me to shoot her a middle finger that made everyone laugh.

Destiny and Angel both gave me a hug and a kiss before they left, and Big Baby and Lil Boy followed them out, which left me and Bone.

"I still want an answer to my previous question," he said.

"What question is that?"

"Where are you sleeping?" he asked.

"Well it seems like we have two empty rooms and four beds to work with. Let's start in here and see who taps out faster, okay?"

Chapter Thirteen
Destiny

When driving a Lamborghini on the highway, it was physically impossible to do the speed limit. You could literally feel the power beneath you and your foot got heavy even if you didn't want it to. Even with me understanding all this, I didn't know what the fuck had possessed me to let Angel drive us, especially since that bitch didn't know the car came with a break petal.

"Angel," I said for the fifth time.

"Relax, bitch, I know what I'm doing," she replied with a laugh.

It took a few deep breaths and a vow not to ever let her get behind the wheel again if we arrived safely to keep me from smacking her ass. I turned to my phone in hopes of finding a distraction on Facebook or Instagram, but instead, what I found was more drama.

"Oh shit," I mumbled.

"What, what's wrong?"

"Hold on. Let me see if I can pull the video up," I said, hoping I wasn't seeing what I thought I was seeing. As soon as it started rolling, I knew there was no need to hope though.

"This nigga is cray-cray for real," I said.

"Who?"

"Deuce. There's a video of this nigga wearing a bright orange bulletproof vest, no shirt, and some basketball shorts, and he's walking through this neighborhood with a choppa and two banana clips. Hold on, there's audio, too," I said adjusting the volume on my phone.

"Monnnnsterrr! Come out and playyyyy," King Deuce sang out.

The next thing you heard was the thunder of gunshots and the rain of hot shells hitting the pavement. Whoever was shooting the video turned in the direction Deuce was firing and you could see niggas running for cover. But an old-school Monte Carlo was obviously the target, and whoever was driving was desperate to get away.

"Well he said he was gonna handle it," Angel said, smiling.

"Yeah, but even he knows better than to go to a neighborhood like a one-man army. He should've just waited until we got back."

"You know he can handle his own wax. Plus he knows how serious this situation with dad is," she replied, cutting across three lanes of traffic to make our exit.

"I'm telling you now, if you wreck this mufucka, you're paying for it," I warned.

"Like I ain't got the money, bitch, please."

It wasn't the money I was worried about. I checked my seat belt to make sure it was still tight, knowing it hadn't loosened in the slightest since I'd checked it ten minutes ago. After verifying that, I hit the play back button to watch the video all over again. I knew this shit had just gone down not too long ago because Instagram hadn't taken it down yet and handed it over to the cops. Deuce's face wasn't exactly clear, but anyone who knew him would know that was definitely his crazy ass pulling the trigger.

I sent him a text, letting him know that there was a video up, and he needed to find out who'd put it up so they could be dealt with. It was understandable that he wanted to make a statement, but shit like this was better than eyewitness's testimony if he had to fight a court case. Deuce lived in a different world governed by rules I didn't understand, but one thing I'd learned from old mob movies was that sometimes you had to kill a mufucka in a loud way to make a statement and send a message. I definitely understood that.

"Nice neighborhood," I said, looking up from my phone to find myself surrounded by million dollar houses.

It was a damn good thing I'd rented a Lambo because not a whole lot of cars would blend in way out here in the middle of this money. We'd made the drive in a couple of hours and it was obvious most people were either still sleep or battling that rush hour traffic to get to work. Either way, the odds were slim that someone was paying attention to us creeping along their tree lined streets.

"This is it," she said, coming to a stop in front of a huge brick structure behind an iron gate.

"Really?" I said, looking at her.

"I know right. How the fuck do we get in there without them knowing we're coming?"

"I don't know, but we can't get her at work either, which means we'll have to snatch her when she's out somewhere," I replied.

"Her husband's a senator and it's election year. When do you think she'll be out alone? We can't wait that long to find out what's going on with dad. I mean, we don't know what they could be doing to him."

I knew she was right, but I hated to admit it. We'd heard countless stories about inmates dying in custody, some from natural causes, but a lot that were suspicious and at the hands of officers. I didn't want my father to be one of those cases.

"Let's go get something to eat and regroup," I suggested. She made a quick U-turn and drove us to an IHOP a few miles away.

"We should've looked for a Waffle House," I said, getting out of the car.

"Do this look like the type of city with a Waffle House? We up here with the white folks, so let's get to these blueberry pancakes," she replied, leading the way.

Once we were inside and seated, I sent Free a text and let her know what the situation was, and I hit up Black Sam to see if the senator had any speaking engagements lined up.

"How you think we should play it?" Angel asked after the waitress took our orders.

"Maybe we should go after him to get to her."

"How you see that working to our benefit?" she asked.

"I'm just freestyling, but this bitch is the assistant director, which means she got some pull, and we could always use that to our advantage. Suppose we don't just ask her for dad's location, but we make her do whatever she gotta do to get him released."

"You think she got that kind of juice? I mean, these are the feds we're talkin' 'bout."

"I think she can get it done, but even if she can't, her husband's a politician and all them mufuckas exist on the art of favors," I replied.

"With those favors comes a certain amount of power. I don't know, sis, making enemies of these type people may not be the smartest move. I mean, this is different from what we're normally involved in."

"It is, but this is for dad. If he ain't worth it then nobody is," I said sincerely.

Her thoughts were in heavy rotation and I understand why. The only way to see victory in any war was to prepare by knowing your enemy first. The world of politics was something we knew very little about, but as children of the ghetto, we understood one undeniable truth. The corruption was beyond comprehension. To even play in that arena meant you had blood on your hands and bodies in your closet, which me and my sisters could understand and relate to. But we did our dirt the old-fashioned way while they did theirs with sleight of hand. That made them more than formidable. That made them more dangerous than us.

"We gotta talk it over with Free," she said.

"Without question, because if we go at it this way then it's gonna take some major fucking planning."

"It's gonna get ugly, though. If we go after these people, then we don't just have to kill them, we have to take care of everyone who gives a damn about them," she said quietly, looking around to see if anyone was paying attention.

I started to respond when the waitress showed up with our pancakes, eggs, and sausage. For a moment, our conversation was put on hold as we got to the business of nourishment because neither of us was the type to play with our food or act like we weren't hungry like some chicks did. The meal may not have been Waffle House certified, but it would do the job. I was halfway through my plate when Free texted me back.

"Free wants us to come back," I said.

"Figures, but it's okay because we need to have this conversation in person anyway."

"My first priority is making sure we get there in one piece, so I'll take those keys," I said, holding my hand out.

"Huh?"

"You heard me, Angel, now hand them over."

"Damn, you petty," she said, trying to turn her lips into a pout, but unable to hide her smile.

"I'll be petty, but I'll be alive and petty," I replied, taking the keys from her.

We finished eating, paid our bill, and got back on the move. Unfortunately, neither of us had been smart enough to think about delaying our return trip because of traffic, and so we were forced to crawl for an hour in bumper to bumper back up.

"Maybe I should've let you drive."

"I wish you had because I would've been hit the service lane and got past this bullshit," she replied, shaking her head.

I was tempted to do just that, but the last thing we needed was to get pulled over because we still had guns in the car. So, we sat. When that gap opened up, though, I had us pushing one hundred and twenty miles per hour before she could get her seat belt on, laughing at how tight she was suddenly gripping the armrest. It was almost eleven a.m. by the time we got back to the motel and now I was definitely tired.

I'd only had time for a short nap yesterday after what had happened with Kimberlee, but she had been worth the sleep deprivation. Thinking about how she'd screamed when I'd taken the knife to her most delicate body parts gave me the chills. Making me wonder if I had a heart at all. I tried telling myself it was just business, but I couldn't deny how business made me feel. When Angel and I walked into our room it was empty, even though both beds looked slept in.

"I got first shower," she said.

"That's cool. I gotta go buy some clothes anyway."

"No, you don't. I brought enough for the both of us," she replied, dumping the contents of her duffle bag on the bed.

Once she had her outfit picked out, she disappeared into the bathroom, leaving me to decide what to wear. I'd just pulled some black jeans and a matching t-shirt from the pile when a knock sounded at the door.

"It's me," Free called out, prompting me to let her in.

"You look better," I said, checking out the Chaka Khan blowout look she was rocking for her hair do and the pep in her step.

"I was able to get a few hours of sleep. Is that Angel in the shower?"

"I damn sure ain't have no time to pick up some stranger, but if I didn't know any better, I'd think you did. You got that freshly fucked glow about you," I replied, watching her closely.

I'd had my suspicions about her and Bone, but I never spoke on it, and the look she was giving me said I didn't need to now.

"Stay focused and tell me how we're getting in this house."

"I don't think that's the right move, but I've got another idea," I said.

We both took seats on the bed and I ran down the conversation Angel and I had over breakfast. There was nothing to be gained by sugar coating shit so I didn't mince words when it came to the apprehension me and Angel felt about putting the squeeze on someone with more power than us. I could tell by the way Free was shaking her head that she understood our fears and wouldn't take them lightly when it came to whatever decision we made.

"So, what do you think?" I asked.

"I think, when it comes to dad, it's always been go big or go home, and we can't go home without him. Right now, we need to keep our options open and keep trying to find out where he's at, but honestly, I think your move might be the best move. If we go that route, there is no pretending like we don't know nothing. We're gonna have to run with him."

"I'd rather be with him than without him," I replied.

"To do this, we're gonna need more help than what we brought with us."

"What are you thinking?" I asked.

"That it's time to go see his homies. I'm gonna arrange a sit down in Chiraq."

Chapter Fourteen
Angel
One week later

When you love someone and they're a big part of your life, you never really get used to them not being there with you. Despite the fact that my dad had been in prison for the last ten years, he was still part of my everyday life because he was only a phone call away. Granted, there was no substitute for his actual presence, but he'd still managed to shape the women me and my sisters were. It never seemed like he was gone, but these last seven days of complete silence brought a reality that was hard to deal with.

I'd never missed my daddy so much in all my life, and to not know where he was or if he was okay forced a feeling of loss and mourning on me that I wasn't prepared for. We used every contact and resource we had, but no one could tell us where the fuck he was. Destiny was blaming herself because she was the one who got the phone in to him, and she wouldn't let the fact that Free told her to do it absolve her in any way. Free had been trying to move with a certain air of detachment about everything, but I knew her, and I knew with each passing day of no answers she got more worried.

We all knew our father could handle his own, that he was cut from a cloth unlike most niggas. He was still human, though. The only way we all knew to avoid getting caught up in our own thoughts about what may or may not be happening was to put our heads down and go to work. Black Sam was based in Florida, but we'd flown her to our temporary base in Maryland so we'd be working shoulder to shoulder in the trenches. She was a four foot eleven inch, black and Irish beauty with the most amazing golden skin tone I'd seen.

Thick in the waist and cute in the face was how Destiny liked them, but Free made it clear that Sam was here to handle the business. After Free's sit-down with the Black Guerilla Family in Chicago, the necessary calls had been made, and we now had the support of all the members worldwide on the mission of finding Father God, and that had given us hope. But after a week of no answers, I was feeling hella discouraged. We ain't never been the type to sit on our hands while other people handle our business, so we'd put our plans into motion.

I still felt some apprehension about what we were gonna pull off, but every day I went without my father, that feeling lessened. From jump we knew that we had to go at this differently than we would an average street nigga, but the basics for any job started with doing your homework. Black Sam hacked into Senator Jordan's email and got a copy of his calendar, which allowed us to know his movements, and she did the same with his wife. We were still trying to make a decision on who to snatch up and ransom for what we wanted, and that would all depend on who could make shit happen quicker.

The senator, Paul Jordan, undoubtedly had pull with the governor of Maryland, but dad wasn't in Maryland anymore, so getting a pardon there wouldn't matter. And we didn't know if the senator had any pull wherever our dad was, or how long it might take to call in the necessary favors. His wife, on the other hand, could make something happen immediately as far as telling us the location, but we were still unsure whether or not she could actually authorize a release.

Before we got to that point, though, we had to take a look at their marriage because our success in kidnapping either of them depended on the love they had for each other. Twenty years was a long time to be with someone. Shit, I'd only been with myself that long and I got on my own damn nerves. While we were digging, though, we did find the one thing the couple had in common, and that was their fourteen-year-old son, Paul Jordan Jr., or PJ, as he was affectionately called. All three of us had always operated with an absence of mercy. Our father had taught us that mercy was a weakness that could and would definitely kill you. It didn't matter if you were eight years old or eighty years old, if you were in our way, then that was your ass and god's plan.

The moment we found out about little PJ, though, I could tell it was gonna be a problem. He didn't live in the big house with his mother and father. He was kept in a facility in Delaware, due to his Autism. It wasn't like they stuck him in there and forgot about him. They visited at least every other weekend and he was allowed to come home sometimes. One of his home visits would be in a couple of days because in an election year, appearances were necessary, and this presented us with all the leverage we needed.

None of us felt good about fucking with a handicapped kid, but being merciful could cost us the one person that meant more than anything in the world. We'd agreed to table the discussion until I got back since I'd been the one to volunteer to go back down south and help KD out. Niggas had been asking not so subtle questions about the bitch who shot Monster's homies ever since I'd signed my plea three days ago. Even though we had enough on our plate, I didn't need these mufuckas going after people I loved or fucking with Freedom's business while we were away. So, I was gonna bring the drama to them hot off the stove like a real bitch would.

I was getting pissed off just thinking about them niggas coming to my city looking for me, and the fact that I had been standing in front of the airport waiting on KD for the past thirty minutes wasn't helping. I'd just pulled my phone out to call him again when my car pulled to the curb in front of me.

"The fuck took you so long?" I asked once I was in the passenger seat.

"Baby mama trippin, you already know. It's good to see you."

"I would say I missed you, but I saw your ass all over the Gram like shit was legal," I replied, inspecting my car to make sure he didn't have any burn marks in the Italian leather or some hoe's drawers in my glove box.

"That shit wasn't my fault. Besides, if the nigga was 'bout that action, he'd stop ducking me and come get what he asked for."

"He ain't gotta come out and play, we'll bring the party to him. I don't like the type of questions he's asking and the heat he's putting on my people."

"I hear you, and I got a plan," he replied, pulling away from the curb.

"Talk to me."

"One of the homies just came home and there's a party for him at the strip club."

"How you know this nigga is gonna show up?" I asked.

"Because the homie that came home is named Lil Monster. They tight, feel me?"

"Where's the party?"

"In Nashville at this new spot called Devil's Playhouse, everything you need is in the bag in the backseat," he said.

I grabbed the backpack off the floor behind the driver's seat and opened it to find a Tech-9 with an extra clip, a red wig, and a black trench coat. Based on those items, the plan was clear to me.

"How am I getting in undetected?" I asked.

"A bitch name Danika I put the dick to is gonna let you in the back. I just gotta call when we get there."

"Bout time your whoring worked to somebody's advantage besides your own," I said, making sure the clip in the gun was loaded and the first round was ready to dance.

"Yeah, whatever, a bitch is always satisfied fucking with me, you hear me?"

I just shook my head and put the gun back in the bag before using my phone to text Free and let her know I had arrived. The plan was to get out of town within a few hours and be back on the road to B-more. It was a long drive, but I was rested.

"You got a ride home?" I asked.

"My homies gonna be around in case a mufucka stumble out the club so I'll catch a ride with them. You want me to take the gun and get rid of it?"

"You know the rules, my nigga. If I put a body on it, then I'ma be the one to make it disappear. Nothing personal, just the business of self-preservation," I replied.

"Yea, yea."

It wasn't like I didn't trust Deuce, because I did. But the rules my father gave me were imbedded in the fiber of my being, and I couldn't go against them. Every move on the streets was life and death, and I saw it for what it was, so I tried to limit the opportunities for mistakes.

"I'ma get something to eat right quick and you can put your wig and shit on," he said, pulling into a McDonald's parking lot.

"Bring me a double cheeseburger," I said, opening the door and stepping out.

The first thing I did was pull up the pants legs on my black sweats so all anyone would see was my ankle running down into my black and red patent leather Jordan's. Sneakers might seem out of place, but most people would think I was resting my feet in between dances because that's what we did. Either way, it didn't matter to me because I wasn't about to try to hit a nigga wearing heels. I put the trench coat on, feeling the strap that had been sewed in, which connected to the inside pocket, and allowed for me to conceal the Tech comfortably under my arm.

Getting back in the car, I flipped the visor down and went about putting the wig on straight, knowing KD must've stolen it from a bitch because most women weren't letting a good wig out they sight. I wasn't from around here, so my simple disguise would be more than effective. The last piece of the puzzle came when I put the handle of the Tech through the strap and tucked it down into the pocket with the extra clip before tying the belt to the jacket at my waist.

"You gonna blend right in," KD said, getting back in the car and passing me the bag of food. I'd only asked for a cheeseburger, but the smell of the hot, salty fries had my mouth watering.

"You sure you wanna eat before doing this?'

"You act like this is my first time. Only my pussy is virginal, my nigga, so shut up and take us to the spot," I said, before stuffing my face with French fries.

It only took us fifteen minutes to get to the club, and it was only a little after ten p.m., but judging by the parking lot, the club was packed.

"What's the layout?" I asked, chewing my sandwich thoroughly.

"It's two floors, one main stage, and a bar. Bunch of tables spread out on the first floor, VIP is upstairs, and it's a balcony scene. When you go in through the back door, you'll have to cross the floor to get to the stairs that take you to the VIP because that's where they'll be at."

"Security?" I asked.

"Bought and paid for, but every nigga with him is probably strapped. You go in there and lay it down and we'll be out here to back you up."

"We?" I asked looking around.

"Yea, my niggas ducked off in that black Expedition sitting in the corner over there," he replied, pointing.

The truck was completely blacked out so I couldn't tell how many people were in it, but hopefully they were ready.

"Call your girl," I said, finishing my burger, and centering my thoughts on what would happen in the next few moments.

He made the call, and two minutes later, the backdoor opened and some light skin chick stuck her head out, her eyes sweeping the parking lot.

"Have my ride parked to make a quick exit," I said, stepping out and going directly to the back door.

Even this far away from the stage, the music was deafening, which could work out in my favor when it came to how quickly everyone reacted to the shots. The girl holding the door took one look at me and signaled for me to follow her. As soon as the door was closed, the familiar scents of sweat, pussy, and liquor punched me in the nose hard, but my mind was focused on where we were going. As soon as we hit the floor, I knew all the cars in the parking lot had been misleading because it was beyond packed in this mu-fucka.

The lighting was dim, except for the spotlight on the main stage, but I could still see niggas and bitches everywhere. I knew the tricks of the trade and I saw some dudes getting lap dances, while others actually had their dicks in the pussy and they were playing it off. Tamika walked me through the maze of people and pointed me in the direction of the stairs leading to the balcony. I didn't pause in stride and no one paid me any attention, but by the time I got halfway up the stairs, I could hear the party going on. I paused once I reached the top and peeked around the corner.

The balcony scene was actually more of a sky box with its own private stripper pole, and there was a girl hanging upside down from it. The little space was packed with both partiers and dancers alike, which meant there was about to be some serious collateral damage. I didn't know what this nigga Monster looked like, but it was obvious who the guest of honor was because he was holding a huge bottle of Ace of Spades and there were three bitches trying to dance on him. All that attention got him nominated because he'd be the first to die.

Pulling the Tech out, I took a deep breath and stepped around the corner like Rambo. Nobody got to scream a warning or push a loved one out the way. No one had time to commune with God or whatever they believed in. Right then and there in the strip club, I made it rain. The life of the party lost his face with my first blast and from there, I just swung side to side like I was waving hello. Part of me felt bad for the chicks these bitch niggas were trying to use as bullet proof vests, but I kept my finger steady on the trigger. It only took seconds before the screaming started and they didn't just come from the balcony, but from downstairs too. I knew I needed to get out during the stampede, but I couldn't let go of the trigger until the clip was empty.

I was tempted to keep going once I'd swapped the full one for the empty, but I'd made my point and it was now time to go. With one hand under my coat, I made my way back downstairs and blended in with the mad rush, careful to keep my eyes open for any threat. Most people were running for the front door, but I turned towards the way I'd come in and I was moving in that direction when I felt my left leg threaten to give out. It was so sudden that I lost my balance and went flying head first into the back door, coming face to face with the pavement of the parking lot.

"Angel,!" Deuce yelled, rushing to pick me up.

I tried to stand, but now I could feel the pain and what happened finally registered to me. I had no idea who did it, but somebody had fucking shot me.

Chapter Fifteen
Freedom

Even the best laid plans had flaws in them. It was just an unavoidable truth about life. Why? Because no one could predict the future. We can't see around corners, and even if we could, the movies have told us that if we see our future, it changes. So, to me that means mistakes will be made, but how do you deal with them dictates your survival. I wasn't the idiot that argues with truth, but right now we couldn't afford any mistakes with this situation because a lot was riding on the outcome. For all the money and power I had, all the connections, but to still come up empty with regards to where my father was being held was disturbing to me.

I don't think I ever underestimated the power of the government, I just don't ever think I understood it. These mufuckas could literally hide a nigga from the world and there wasn't a damn thing you could do about it. But something had to be done because I wasn't losing my dad, not without one helluva fight.

"What's shakin', Black Sam?" I asked, answering the knock on my motel room door.

Since we were gonna be in town for a while we'd gotten her a room in line with ours and she'd set up shop with three different laptops she'd brought with her.

"Looks like there's been some changes," she replied, stepping into the room and going to the table where she could show me her findings on her laptop.

"What's new?"

"Well, for starters, the senator has cancelled all public speaking engagements for the next week. And there's a Sprinter van coming to pick him up in a few hours and take him out of town."

"Where to?" I asked.

"Delaware."

We both knew what that meant, but it was a surprise because he wasn't supposed to bring his son home for another few days.

"What about the wife?" I asked.

"Nothing has changed with her yet and she's at work today. It looks like he's gonna surprise her."

I let those revelations turn over in my mind as I looked for a way to capitalize on them. Since mistakes were inevitable, should I see this as the senator's mistake, or my good luck? I'd probably see it as good luck if I was prepared to make a move, but Angel was out of town handling her business. If I waited, though, then the whole family could be locked up in that house for another week, and that's another week of me being in the dark about my dad. I damn sure wasn't trying to do that.

Truthfully, this wasn't a decision I could make on my own, though, so I pulled my phone out and sent a group text to have everyone come to my room. It only took a few minutes before mufuckas was beating the door down.

"A'ight, here's the situation. The senator has cleared his schedule and he's going to pick up his son in a few hours. What that means is we have the option now to beat him to the punch or possibly wait another week because that's how long he cleared his schedule for."

"We gotta make our move now then," Destiny said.

"Without Angel, though?" Bone asked.

"I don't like that idea either, but if we miss this opportunity who knows when we'll find our father. The time is now," Destiny replied, empathetically,

The look Bone was giving me was basically asking if I agreed with him or my sister. I already knew that Big Baby would side with Destiny and Lil Boy would follow whatever his brother wanted to do. I saw both sides of the coin, I just hoped I was making the right decision.

"If we're gonna do this, we gotta plan it now because our window of opportunity is dumb small. Black Sam, what time is his ride coming to get him?" I asked.

"It's scheduled for seven p.m. and the trip should take about three to four hours."

"We can make better time than that with the cars we're driving," Destiny said.

"Okay, so what makes the most sense, going after the boy before his dad can get there or taking him from his dad?" I asked.

"Well, when you think about it, that's the difference between attacking an entire facility or going after a few cars," Bone said.

"Is he taking any type of security with him?" Destiny asked.

"He's a senator, not the president," Black Sam replied.

"Then we hit the Sprinter van. We're gonna need fast cars that won't trace back to us, and masks, so I'ma get in touch with dad's homies to run down on them," I ordered.

"Masks and untraceable cars? Killers don't wear masks and they damn sure don't hide, so why all the unnecessary trouble?" Destiny asked.

"Because it is necessary. We're not about to kill the senator right now, we're getting ready to bring a parent's nightmare to life. Shit like that will make folks desperate, and if he knows who we are, he might try to send someone at us before what we ask for is done. Will he speculate that it's us? Sure, at some point, but his first instinct is gonna be to find out about dad, and that leads directly to his affiliation. The Black Guerilla Family has a strong presence in Maryland, and that'll be the first place the senator looks, which buys us time. Lastly, when it's all said and done, me, you, and Angel will be on the run, but that doesn't mean everybody who helped us has to be. So, we're gonna pull this off as anonymously as possible, okay?" I said looking at everyone in the room.

I could feel Bone's eyes on me when I'd said something about me and my sisters being on the run, and I knew his thoughts were centered on the fact that he hadn't been included. It wasn't fair of me to do that to him, though. This life was the life I'd chosen and I had no right to ask him to do the same. I knew eventually we'd have a conversation about all of this shit, but right now we had to pay attention to the task in front of us.

"I'ma make the necessary calls while you all get ready," I said, taking my phone and going outside.

I casually strolled around the motel keeping my eyes open for anything resembling a threat while arranging for everything we'd need, including a safe house to stash the boy in. It was beyond short notice, but I was confident these niggas could get everything done, especially since they had so much love for my father. By the time I'd made a full lap around the motel, I was assured everything would be taken care of within the hour. Heading back to my room, I pulled up short at the sight of Bone waiting for me out front by my car.

"What's up?" I asked.

"We need to talk."

"I know that, but now really ain't the time."

"When is the time, Free, when you're already on the run?" he asked, clearly frustrated.

"What do you want me to say, Bone? I'm trying to save my father's life and return him to his rightful position."

"Baby, I get that, and I've been riding with you the whole time, so why exclude me now?" he asked, reaching for my hand and pulling me right in front of him.

"Because I can't ask you to give up everything you know and love for me."

"But it wouldn't just be for you it would be for us. All of us."

"What do you mean all of us?" I asked slowly. The look he gave me went beyond the surface, it felt like he was looking at my soul for a moment.

"Freedom, I know you. I know you better than you know yourself sometimes, and I definitely pay attention to you."

"Okay," I replied, somewhat confused.

"I know your body, too. When was the last time you had a period?"

My first instinct was to laugh his question off, but suddenly my brain started doing rapid calculations and I felt horror descending over me.

"I-I can't be," I whispered.

"We both know how regular you are, Free. Think about it."

I opened my mouth to speak, but I couldn't find the words. To speak the words meant I had to accept a truth I wasn't ready to deal with.

"I-I can't think about this right now, I've gotta focus on what we're getting ready to do," I said, taking a step back from him.

"Not thinking about it won't make it go away, and not finishing this conversation won't make me go away. I may not have told you enough, but I love you, Freedom, and because of that love, I'll follow you to the end of the earth."

The sincerity in his eyes brought a wave of emotions to the surface and I had to fight to keep myself from crying. Now wasn't the time and this wasn't the place, but I couldn't fight the urge I had to kiss him, and I did just that. Any questions he had, I answered them in the moment with pure, unchecked passion, not caring who saw us.

"I love you, too," I said, taking his hand and leading him back to the motel room.

"Free, I think I have what you're looking for," Sam said as soon as we came through the door.

"I think she's got what she's looking for," Destiny teased, smiling at me.

"Shut it, bitch, we've got work to do," I replied, smiling.

"Okay so the facility where PJ is at is located in a rural section of Claymont, Delaware, and it was built on a few hundred acres of farm land. The security at the actual facility is good, but not so much for the surrounding property because nothing ever happens in that part of the world. There's only one road in and one road out, and if someone were to be lurking in the woods, they could definitely get a drop on an unsuspecting senator," Sam concluded, pulling up a GEO map of the facility and everything surrounding it. I could easily see what she was talkin' about, and that gave me confidence in our next move.

"A'ight, let's get ready to do this," I said.

Big Baby went to his and Lil Boy's room and came back with the duffel bag of guns they'd rode with up here. Everyone except Black Sam got handed a Glock .19 with an extra clip. Big Baby and Lil Boy each had a Mac-11. Bone had an HK-MP5. Destiny went with an AK-47, and I, of course, had my trusty Mossberg pump. Bone also made a quick trip to his room and came back with a bulletproof vest for me.

"Where's mine?" Destiny asked, screwing her face to create her best look of being offended.

I wasn't paying attention to her, though, because I was reading the message Bone was telegraphing with his eyes, knowing neither of us could put into words the fear we felt for what we might be jeopardizing. I could be pregnant, but I couldn't let that stop what had to be done. Focusing on our next move, we went over who was riding with who, what cars would be used to box them in, and who would hop out to rush the Sprinter van. We knew we had to move fast to avoid giving the senator time to call for help, which meant the driver would have to be taken care of a.s.a.p. After we got what we came for, we just had to hope that his parents loved him enough to want him back by any means.

"Sam, I want you to have a message ready to go to Tracy Jordan that says we have her son and her husband has our demands, and that if she contacts anyone besides her husband about this then her son dies. Once we actually have him, then you can send it," I said.

"So, you want me to monitor her communications, email, phone, twitter, and Facebook?"

"Definitely, and keep me posted about the slightest thing you find suspicious."

Our plan was simple and thrown together in a hurry, but that didn't mean it wouldn't work just how we needed it to. Forty-five minutes later, I got a text with the address of a safe house we'd be using in Oxen Hill, Maryland, and there were three cars with the keys in them in the parking lot. I looked out the window and sure enough there was a black Nissan 300ZX, a dark blue Chevy Avalanche, and a black Mazda RX-7. Speed and transport.

"It's show time," I said.

Black Sam was staying put, but the rest of us gathered everything we needed and chose a ride. Naturally, Big Baby and Lil Boy took the truck, and Destiny decided she wanted the RX-7 so Bone and I took the 300ZX. He didn't waste any time getting on the road, moving with the precision and speed of a fast and furious movie. There was so much I wanted to say to Bone, and I could've spoke freely, but our survival depended on us being one-hundred percent focused on what we had to do. Still, we held hands the entire ride, communicating through touch all that was understood without words. Even though we had a head start, we were still racing against time because we had to get there and be in position so nothing seemed out of the ordinary.

An hour into our drive, Black Sam called to let me know Senator Jordan was on the move, which made me put my foot down harder on the gas pedal. It still took us another hour and a half to get there, but we arrived under the cover of night, and that would come in handy if witness testimony became an issue. The country roads attached to the piece of land were narrow and winding, and that allowed for it only taking one car or truck to block off travel.

Me, Bone, Lil Boy, and Big Baby posted up in a turn-off that was almost completely out of sight and Destiny went further down past the facility so she could be behind the van when they left. The plan was to box them in, make our move, and be like the wind. For me, the hardest part was waiting because I was ready to do this. It was close to two hours before I heard the sound of gravel being crushed by a large vehicle, and then the Mercedes van drove right past us.

I shot Destiny a text and then I pulled the bulletproof vest over my t-shirt before pulling my hoodie over that. Our supplier hadn't missed any details because in each ride there had been clown masks, and Bone and I put ours on then.

"You ready?" he asked.

"Don't coddle me because you think I'm pregnant, nigga, you know this is what I do," I replied, pulling the shotgun up from beside me where I'd had it wedged against the door.

I couldn't see his face, but I knew the smirk he had on it by the snickering laughter. He was lucky I loved his ass. It was damn near thirty or more minutes before Destiny texted to say they were moving towards us, but we were ready. Big Baby pulled the truck broad side across the road, and him and Lil Boy hopped out to wait with the trees on one side of the road while we took the other side. Just as Bone and I stepped into the shadows, I saw lights bouncing off of trees and I heard the van approaching. Within seconds, I heard the breaks lock up as the van skidded to a stop inches from the side of the truck.

The driver had that 'what the fuck' look on his face, but it quickly turned to terror when Lil Boy stepped out of the night and pressed the barrel of his MAC to the driver side window. Immediately, the driver's door was opened and then the back-passenger door slid open, revealing a frail looking boy in a wheel chair. Naturally, the senator stepped forward and he opened his mouth to speak, but my shotgun answered all his questions at first glance.

"How this plays out all depends on you. Your son's life is in yours and your wife's hands."

Chapter Sixteen
Destiny

It didn't take more than one-hundred and eighty seconds for us to get in and get out, but the job wasn't done because we still had to make it to safety. Once Big Baby and Lil Boy had PJ in the truck, I pulled my car around the van and we hit the road while Bone and Free explained the rules of engagement. Once we reached the main road, I got in front of the truck so if the cops wanted to pull someone over, they'd get me first. As soon as we got on the highway, I treated that RX-7 like it was my rented Lambo and I pushed it to the limit.

A couple times I had to ease up and wait for Big Baby to get back in sight of me, but we were still moving. It wasn't until Free texted me that I took a deep breath and actually allowed myself to think about what this might mean if we pulled this shit off. I knew firsthand that there was nothing in the world my daddy wouldn't do for me, and if PJ's parents felt the same way, then the clock was ticking on when I got my father back. Just the thought of him being out had me smiling so hard that my cheeks were hurting. I was so wrapped up in my thoughts that I almost didn't answer my phone, but seeing Angel's number made me happier because I could give her the good news.

"What's up, sis. I got some tea for you, bitch," I said.

"This ain't Angel, it's Deuce."

"Deuce? Nigga, why you calling me from my sister's phone?" I asked. His response wasn't immediate and I felt the tingling of fear because Deuce wasn't quiet or at a loss for words.

"Vontae, what's going on?" I asked seriously.

"It's Angel. Some shit cracked off and she got shot in the leg, but she is a'ight."

I heard a loud buzzing echoing through my head, and for a minute, the road in front of me waved like a mirage in the desert. He had spoken plain English and his words made sense, but the shit wasn't computing. I know goddamn well he didn't say my big sister got shot.

"The fuck you just say? Repeat that one more time, nigga."

"Listen, she good, I promise. The bullet went straight through and she's getting sewed up now," he replied in an attempt to soothe me.

"You let my fucking sister get shot?" I screamed into the phone, wishing I could magically appear wherever the hell he was.

"It wasn't my fault. It was a misunderstanding with security and somebody was there who wasn't supposed to be."

"My nigga, are you seriously making excuses right now? You know you can get your shit pushed back, too," I warned.

"Look, I'm taking care of Angel, and as soon as she finished getting stitched up, she's gonna call you. Don't tell Free, though."

"Say what? Don't tell Free? You must be smoking and drinking," I said getting more pissed off by the minute.

"Y'all got some serious shit going on and she don't need that type of stress. I'll bring Angel home and take care of her because you know that her being hurt means she can't get down with the move right now."

I didn't wanna admit that he was right, but he was. It would've been difficult enough to have her up here with a bullet wound, even if we hadn't pushed up our schedule. We were in the mix now and it was best for her to be on the sideline until we had all the loose ends tied up. The only question was how could I keep some shit like this from Freedom?

"As soon as Angel gets her leg sewn up, I want her to call me, understand?"

"I got you," he replied, hanging up.

Free was gonna go ape shit when she found out we were keeping something this major from her, but hopefully having our father home would lessen the storm. It was hard to process Angel being shot and us not being by her side to offer whatever support she needed, even if it was only a hug. We had to stay focused, though. The journey back to Maryland took a full three hours, but we all arrived at the safe house in one piece and without a wall of cops collapsing on us. As hard as it was gonna be, I knew I had to avoid Free because she would know I was hiding something.

"Why don't we take shifts?" I suggested once we were all locked into the ground floor apartment in the middle of the projects.

"Shifts? Why? You got somewhere to go?" Free asked, unfolding the wheel chair so Big Baby could sit PJ down.

"Nah, I'm just saying we still have more shit to do, and it don't take all of us to watch a handicapped kid. Did Black Sam send that message?"

"Yea, and I made sure to fill the senator in for what we wanted. They've got a twelve-hour window before pieces of the young boy are delivered. One thing we do need to take care of is the plane and cleaning out our motel rooms. Do you wanna handle that?" she asked.

"I can, and I'll take Big Baby and Lil Boy with me to get all our cars."

"Okay, I'll message Black Sam and tell her to start packing shit up and wiping shit down," she said, pulling out her phone.

After getting the keys from her and Bone, I motioned for Big Baby and Lil Boy to follow me, and we all piled into the truck for the ride back out to Baltimore. I chose to sit in the backseat so I could text Angel while I was checking on how to set a date and flight time for the open-ended rental we had on the G3. Freedom said she gave them twelve hours, which put it at ten or eleven a.m. tomorrow, so I requested the plane be fueled and ready to go from BWI by noon. But we only had one stop to make and then it was off into the sunset. My text to Angel was to let her and Deuce know that he needed to get on the road with her tonight and get her up here or her ass was left behind.

Of course, we wouldn't really leave her, but I said it to light a fire under their ass. I was feeling some type of way because there was too much going on at once and there were no signs that shit was gonna slow down. I mean, after tomorrow, everything would change, and nothing would be the same again. Part of me wanted to embrace that change with all my heart because I dreamed of the day it would happen, but the other part of me was hella nervous. I knew how I wanted things to be, but I didn't know what to expect.

"I know all this shit is happening really fast and the odds are good that tomorrow I'll be out of this country, but without sounding mushy, I wanted you to know I love you," I said. I saw Big Baby exchange a look with Lil Boy before Lil Boy turned to look at me.

"We love you, too, with your sentimental ass," he replied, laughing.

"Fuck you, negro."

"Even if you did take dick, you couldn't take this one," he said, laughing harder. All I could do was shake my head because he was damn sure telling the truth.

"That shit ain't legal, bruh-" My phone interrupted my smartass comment and I answered it with the quickness because it was Angel's number.

"Deuce?"

"No, it's me," she replied.

"Thank God! Are you okay? Bitch, if you die, I'ma kill you!"

"Yea I'm okay, and I ain't gonna die from a leg shot," she said, laughing softly.

"Don't act like it can't happen because there are arteries in your legs and if one got hit you can bleed to death.

"Well don't worry because I only got hit in my calf."

"What the fuck happened, Angel?" I asked, getting mad all over again.

"We don't really need to talk about that on the phone, but I would like you to explain the sudden travel plans real quick."

"An opportunity presented itself and we had to make a move. You should already know what I'm talking about."

"I do, but is everything straight?" she asked.

I could hear the hope in her voice and I knew what she was envisioning. We all I had fantasies of our dad walking out of those prison Gates and us right there waiting on him. It might not exactly go down like that because we would have to reunite in secret, but it wouldn't take away from the magic of having him back.

"Everything is moving according to plan, which is why you need to be headed in this direction, feel me?"

"A'ight. I'm on some pretty good dope so I'm not feeling the pain, and I got my car-"

"Driving would take too long. Just hop on the next flight out," I said.

"Damn, it's going down that fast? Okay, I'ma get Deuce to drive me to the airport and I'll text you with my flight time."

"Good shit. Be safe and I love you."

"Love you, too," she replied, disconnecting.

"Did we just hear your conversation right? Did Angel get shot?" Lil Boy asked.

"Yea, but Free don't know."

The look he gave me said that he wouldn't wanna be the one keeping that kind of secret from my sister, and even though I agreed, I still had no choice. It took us an hour to get back to the motel, but luckily for us, Black Sam already had two of the four rented rooms wiped down. They probably hadn't been that clean since the motel first opened. I helped her go through the other two rooms and erase all evidence of our existence while Big Baby and

Lil Boy loaded up the guns and the clothes we'd travelled with. It took damn near an hour before we were ready to go.

"You ever drove a Lamborghini?" I asked Sam.

"Nope."

"Well you're about to because it's not safe for you to drive Free's car. Don't misunderstand, if you wreck the Lambo, I'ma kick your ass and you're still gonna pay for the car. If you were to wreck Free's car, she'd probably kill you," I informed her.

"I understand, and I don't wanna drive her car," she replied, eagerly taking the keys I offered.

Once everybody was loaded up, we got back on the road. With Angel taking a flight back up here, that only gave me a few hours to find a way to tell Free about her being shot. In my mind, I was thinking I should just spit it out and take the tongue lashing I was gonna get, but on the other hand, I could say nothing and let Angel do the talking. I liked that idea better the more I thought about it. As soon as my phone started ringing, I knew it was Free because there was no way my luck could hold out about her being in the dark about Angel's shooting.

"Yea?" I answered.

"Where are you?"

"We're just getting on the road to come back to you," I replied, sensing the excitement in her voice.

"Don't come here, we'll come to you so we can be close to the airport. I know where he is and they're arranging his release for tomorrow morning. Bitch, dad is coming home!"

Chapter Seventeen
Angel

The feeling of butterflies in my stomach was something I hadn't experienced before, and I wasn't sure how to feel about it. I was nervous, and I never got nervous, but it was understandable because if what Destiny said was true, we were about to get our dad back. I knew that no matter my age, I'd always be his little girl, but I was a woman now and for him that would be an adjustment. I couldn't stop the questions swimming through my mind about whether he would approve of us and the way we lived our lives.

I mean, when he was locked down, he was more or less forced to accept it, but being on the streets meant he could directly affect change. Knowing that was part of what was making me nervous. That didn't overshadow my happiness, though, because a bitch was somewhere past the moon, and it wasn't just the pain pill I'd popped.

"Your sister still threatening to kill me?" KD asked, coming out the kitchen with a bottle of Apple Ciroc in his hand.

I didn't know whose little rundown apartment. We were in, but I'd woke up right where I was laying on this lumpy sofa that smelled like good weed. The carpet was thin and missing in spots, and the only other furniture was a matching beige love seat and a flat screen T.V. sitting on top of an antique floor model in the corner. It served its purpose, though, because it was a safe haven in my time of need.

"She didn't mention killing you, but whenever Free finds out, that's a different story."

"I know. Here, you gonna need this for the ride so the pain don't hit you in the face," he said, handing me the bottle.

"The ride won't be that long, but I'll drink some on the way to the airport."

"Airport? I thought you wanted to have your car and not leave no evidence when you blew town?" he asked.

"That was the plan, but apparently shit is moving faster than I thought and I gotta get back up top a.s.a.p. If everything goes right for us, you can keep the car, bruh. I ain't trippin'."

"That's what's up. when you need to be at the airport?"

In response to his question, I went back to my phone to check departure times for flights going to BWI or Regan national airport. It was a risk simply because, if for some reason I came under suspicions, there would be questions of why I flew in and out so quickly, but travelling was still legal in this country, so they'd need more than that to come for me. As my luck would have it there was a flight leaving in forty minutes, and the next one wasn't until six a.m.

"Can you get me to the airport to make a flight in forty minutes?"

"With time to spare. Let me go get the car," he said, heading for the front door.

While he was doing that, I paid for my ticket and sent Destiny a text to let her know I'd be there soon, but I really wanted to call Free and find out exactly what the deal was. I didn't like not being in the loop, and for them to make a move without me even before I'd gotten shot meant shit was real. For all I knew my father could be there waiting on me when I landed. Just the thought of that had that nervous energy flowing through me again. But in my heart, I knew there was no need for it.

My father's love had never went away or waivered in the slightest just because he went to prison. He'd made sure we felt his presence and that had always kept us full of hope, even though we knew that hope alone wouldn't be enough. If you wanted something in this world, you had to be prepared to take it, and take what came behind it. Sometimes your only options were either to pray or to prey, and no middle ground would suffice. Once I got on that plane, I would be one step closer to receiving everything I'd sacrificed for, and I couldn't put into words how bad I was looking forward to that.

"You ready?" KD asked, coming through the door.

Putting my phone in my pocket, I gently pushed up off the couch, making sure to put my weight on my right leg. Before I could take a step, he was at my side, putting my arm around his shoulder so I could lean on him for support. It was slow going, but he got me in the passenger seat then ran back to get my liquor before he got behind the wheel.

"Get you a sip, you sweatin' already," he said.

Just moving my leg a little sent an echo of pain through my body, and I could tell already I was gonna be chasin' pills with Ciroc before too long. Cracking the seal on the bottle, I took a healthy gulp that made my eyes water, but I took a deep breath and tipped the bottle again.

"I said a sip, you ain't tryin' to get lit before you get on the plane," he said.

"I'm good, bruh, just stop and get me another sandwich or something."

"I got you," he replied, starting the car and pulling off.

I took one more hit of the liquor and screwed the top back on. Pulling the visor down so I could look in the mirror gave me a surprise I wasn't ready for because a bitch was looking rough. My eyes were somewhat puffy and the ponytail I'd been rocking under the wig was all types of fucked up.

"Where'd you put the wig?" I asked, fixing my ponytail.

"Everything is in the bag," he said, nodding towards the backseat.

"You didn't think I looked good as a red head?"

"You'd look good bald, you hear me? But some people saw you get shot and I didn't want them to identify you."

"You still ain't told me who the fuck shot me because wasn't nothing moving when I left the VIP," I said.

"It wasn't none of them niggas. It was a mufuckin security guard that wasn't supposed to be working. I think he saw you lay shit down. I mean, I would've asked him, but once he got outside, I peeled his shit back."

"Did I get the nigga Monster?" I asked.

"Did you? Ain't nothing walk up out of there. I'm telling you, your body count was at least twenty."

It didn't make me feel good that some of that number had been women in the same profession as me. There was no justifying it, and I wouldn't try. But at least I'd gotten what I came for and eliminated that threat.

"You're welcome, my nigga, just consider that my going away present to you," I said.

"You ain't coming back, huh?" he asked, more serious than I'd heard him in a while.

It had always been me and my sisters, but King Deuce was my brother that the streets had provided. Real niggas were hard to find in this day and age, but loyal real niggas were almost unheard of, and it was this that I'd missed the most.

"If my sisters are doing what I think they're doing, then the ends of the earth might not be far enough for us to run to. There's no going back."

"Your pops must be a helluva nigga to make y'all do all that."

"I can't put it into words," I told him honestly.

There wasn't one thing that defined a real nigga, it was a multitude of experiences, choices, and maybe a few regrets. FatherGod was everything that embodied.

"Just call a nigga sometime so I know y'all good," he said, pulling into the Burger King parking lot.

"You ain't even gotta ask that, you know what it is."

"What you want to eat?" he asked.

By now I was feeling the mixture of the Ciroc and the Percs in my system, so I really wasn't hungry, but if I didn't eat, I'd probably throw up and I didn't want that.

"Just get me a Whopper and some fries. Oh, and a ginger ale if they got it."

As he was getting out the car, my phone vibrated and I pulled it out to find a text from Destiny with a bunch of crying smiley face emoji's. I felt my stomach drop for what this might mean, but I didn't wanna get my hopes up without being absolutely sure. I sent her an immediate response asking if the nightmare was over, knowing that she would know exactly what that meant. I knew I was breathing, but it still felt like I was holding my breath waiting on her to hit me back.

They said a watched pot doesn't boil so I sat my phone in my lap and tried to focus on anything other than it, and that's when I saw them. When KD had pulled into the parking lot, he'd driven around to the side of the restaurant, so when he parked, I had a clear view inside of the counter and the people eating. There was only a few people given what time it was, but even in a crowd, these niggas would stick out. I caught sight of them as they were creeping through the front door, masked up, and choppa's out.

Both of them had on all black hoodies with matching pants and nothing about them was identifiable, except their intentions because niggas moving like that had one thing in mind. Murder. My mind was already moving before coherent a thought registered because all of a sudden, the backpack was in my hands and I was clawing at the zipper. I was hoping that the wig wasn't the only thing KD put back in this mufucka, and I wasn't disappointed. Grabbing the TECH-9, I opened my door and pushed through the pain to get out of the car in a hurry. As soon as my feet were planted, the shooting started and I looked through the window in time to see KD diving over the counter while the overhead menu rained on him.

There was no way I'd make it inside the restaurant in time to stop them from knocking my nigga's brains loose, which only left one option. As fast as my legs would carry me, I made it up onto the side walk, racked the slide, and let that bitch breathe. The barrel of the TECH was glowing like a million candles at a visual, making the picture window disappear along with one of the niggas trying to kill KD. The other one ducked behind the booth, but I didn't take my finger off the trigger. When that TECH talked to you, your survival instincts made you wanna talk back, and when my clip was empty, I saw dude pop up ready to do just that.

The problem was he forgot about KD. The moment he poked his head out, a single .45 shot rang his bell for the final time and KD came running in my direction.

"Get in," he yelled. Hopping back into the car, I flung myself into the passenger seat in time to catch the bag he was throwing at my head.

"Fuck is this?"

"Your damn food! I paid for that shit so I grabbed it on the way out," he replied starting the car and peeling out of the parking lot.

The fact that he had the presence of mind to grab my damn food after we'd just chopped two niggas down was amazing to me. This mufucka was crazy with capital letters. I heard my phone vibrating, but I couldn't see it because it was on the floor. Bending down, I swept my hand back and forth until I felt it, but when I stuck my head back up, there were blue lights flashing everywhere.

"Oh shit," I mumbled, knowing that the odds of me getting out of this were slim, considering the fact I literally couldn't run.

Before I could look to KD and ask what we were going to do, I was thrust back into the seat as my car demonstrated its ability to giddy-up.

"Can you outrun them?" I asked, looking in my side mirror to see how far back the two cop cars were.

"I don't got a choice," he replied, swerving around the car in front of us and blowing through a red light.

We had a nice lead on the cops, but it was evident that they weren't giving up. Using my shirt, I began to wipe down every part of the TECH-9.

"Hit a corner so I can get rid of this mufucka," I said, winding my window down.

I knew he was heading for the highway, but he made a few quick turns to give me time to toss the gun out the window while he did the same thing. Dumping the gun made me feel a little better, but that feeling was short lived because all of a sudden, the night was lit up all around us.

"Helicopter," he said looking at me.

The look in his eyes said it all. We both knew that you could outrun a lot of things, but that eye in the sky wasn't one of them. He made a hard left and we fishtailed around a corner only to come face to face with a road block, which meant we had no choice except to stop. As we skidded to a stop my phone vibrated again and I looked at the text message. And I cried.

Chapter Eighteen
Freedom

Time never seemed to go as slow as when you wanted it to fly. Ever since I'd gotten the word that my father's release was being arranged, the minute hand on any clock I looked at seemed to be mocking me. Even the drive back to the motel seemed faster than I remembered, but I didn't feel any closer to what I wanted. Was I nervous? The thought of feeling that way was completely alien to me so I wasn't sure if my constant change in thought, pacing, and loss of appetite were symptoms.

I was definitely out of sorts, though, and even Bone had noticed that. He didn't know what to do, and he was scared to make any suggestions after my response to his idea that I take a pregnancy test while we had time to kill. I still didn't know what possessed this nigga to even come out his mouth with some shit like that, knowing the pressure already on my shoulders because of what was at stake. I'd had to cuss him out, that was something he earned.

After I calmed down, I felt a little bad, though, because I knew he just wanted to know if he was gonna be a daddy. He had a right to know that, but I couldn't face the reality of motherhood at the moment, so all that would have to be put on hold. Right now, my focus was on anticipating any bullshit. It was obvious the senator understood how serious the situation was because the fact that he was producing results this fast showed his motivation.

He loved his son, and the boy loved him too because he hadn't given us any problems that would get him killed. Somehow, I thought he was evaluating everything as more cool than dangerous because he probably never considered his dad important enough for some shit like this to happen. To keep him calm, I'd explained it like something of an adventure he'd never forget. When Big Baby came back to pick him up from the safe house, I'd even let him sit in the front seat of the truck to demonstrate my trust in him to act right. I'd gotten him set up in a room with Destiny and ordered him pizza while Black Sam went to the store on a junk food run.

For a hostage, PJ was getting the royal treatment, and I'd even let him send his dad a video so he could tell him that. Destiny thought that was crazy, but I knew it would motivate Senator Jordan because he knew how quickly the tide could change. I was tempted to contact him now to see what progress he'd made, but I wouldn't be satisfied with anything other than my father's release and I'd see anything other than that as excuses. No need to piss myself off, I just had to be patient.

"You need to get some sleep," Bone said.

"I'm not tired."

"Yes, you are, but you're still up on pure adrenaline."

I stopped my pacing in front of the bed he was laying on. We didn't have the lights or T.V. on in the room, and the curtains were closed, but I didn't need to see him to see the look he was giving me. I stared at him for a few more seconds and then I resumed my slow pacing from the front door to the bathroom door and back.

"You need your rest, Free," he said softly.

"I need to think."

"That's all you been doing is thinking. There are too many variables for you to plan for everything that could happen or go wrong. You've just gotta do the best you can."

"And what if that's not enough? We've come too far to fail," I said.

"You won't fail. We won't fail. But you know like I do that shit is about to get realer than it's been, and you can't be on top of your game or thinking straight without rest."

I knew he was right, but I damn sure didn't have to like it. I wanted to give my mind a rest, but it wasn't like I could hit a button and power down like some machine. Maybe if I kept pacing I'd eventually have to give in to exhaustion.

"Tell me what's on your mind," he said, sitting up.

"Everything! Where is he? What time will he be released? How do we go about the exchange without getting caught? Is there a trap? I mean, there's so much to think about. And where do we go when it's over? How long before the senator figures out it was me and my sisters who pulled the whole thing off?"

"Babe, you've covered your tracks, and you know he's gonna choose the obvious villain in this scenario, which is your dad's affiliates. As for the exchange, only you can set the terms on that because you have the leverage and that means you call the shots. How do you wanna do it?" he asked.

That was a question I'd been asking myself for the better part of the last two hours. I knew I had to be smart about this, but I didn't wanna overthink it or overanalyze. I needed to trust my instincts.

"I think we need to rent another plane because if we send the same one to get him wherever he is to fly out of the country we might not make it off the tarmac. They're gonna trace his movements, but we only need to keep them off our trail long enough to get into a non-extradition country."

"Which country?" he asked.

"I've given that a lot of thought because my original idea was Brazil, but then I started thinking that it needed to be somewhere the U.S Government won't come, and won't have successful negotiations with. The only place that makes sense is Moscow."

"Russia? Damn, that's real life. But do you really think we've gotta go that far, babe?"

"If we gotta kill PJ, then yeah," I replied softly.

I'd put a lot of people in the ground, and most of that came without remorse because they either had it coming or they were in my way. I didn't relish the thought of killing this kid though. I would if I had to, but I was hoping his parents wouldn't force my hand.

"When the charter company opens up, I'll rent another plane, which means we only gotta figure out where and how to do the exchange," he said. I stopped pacing and went to stand in front of him.

"You don't have to do this, Bone, you don't have to give up your whole life."

I felt his hands on my hips and he was pulling me closer until his hands were pressed right against my stomach.

"My whole life is with you," he whispered tenderly.

In that moment, I was thankful for the darkness so he couldn't see my tears because I wasn't sure I could explain them. This man had been my right arm in the game that said you couldn't trust a soul. He didn't just have my back he'd become my spine and kept me upright no matter what. He'd shown me what real was, and it touched my heart that he was still down to do that, knowing how fucked up shit would get.

My hands went to his head as I felt him push my shirt up and softly kiss my stomach. Those kisses started out innocently, but when he unbuttoned my pants and continued kissing along my panty line, I felt heat starting at my toes. I didn't object when he pulled both my pants and panties down or when he pushed my t-shirt over my head. Even in the shadows, I could feel his hungry eyes tracing my silhouette, seeing every inch of me that was imprinted on his memory.

The feeling of his rough hands on my ass as he was pulling me closer started a steady throb between my thighs, and when his teeth grazed my nipple, I quit breathing for a second. He teased the left one with his tongue and teeth before moving to the right, and nowhere in between could I find a steady breath to take. Suddenly he stood up and I could feel his presence, his shadow looming over me, but it gave me a feeling of protection instead of fear.

Reaching out, I took ahold of his shirt and pulled it off him before making quick work of his jeans so we could both have the same thing on. He was gentle when taking my face in his hands, but his kiss was possessive and demanding, full of passion. If love ever had a taste, it was on his tongue in this moment because I swore he was kissing me from his soul. When I tried to push him backwards onto the bed, I met resistance and immediately his hand went to my throat. I opened my mouth to speak, but I was spun around and bent over before I could utter a word.

When he pushed inside me, I was forced to put my arms out and brace myself on the bed or go flying over it, but I loved it. His moans were involuntary and I knew they came from how tight and wet my pussy was.

"I'ma make you cum," I warned.

"You first," he replied, grabbing two handfuls of my juicy ass and feeding me them long, back-breaking strokes.

He wasn't going fast, and he was hitting every sweet spot on his travels, making it harder to breathe than before. The way his dick throbbed in rhythm to the beat of my pussy had my whole body singing and wanting to fly.

"I-I want- I want it," I moaned, throwing it back at him.

I knew he couldn't take the way my walls were squeezing him without responding, so I kept doing it until I felt him diving faster and harder. When his hands moved from my ass to my hips, I knew the rough ride was beginning. The feeling of his fingers digging into my skin as our bodies collided over and over awoke the animal in me, forcing my moans of passion to entwine with the growls of savage want.

"Fuck! Fuck me-fuck me like you mean it," I screamed, knowing he had to accept the challenge to his ego.

And accept the challenge he did, making me cum so hard my arms gave out, which forced me on my neck, but he didn't miss a stroke.

"T-talk shit now," he growled through clenched teeth, putting one leg up on the bed and continuing his onslaught of powerful blows.

I couldn't scream or talk shit. All I could do was take his beautiful punishment and cum all over him again. At the height of my orgasm, I felt him join me right before we completely collapsed on the bed together, both of us fighting for air. It was clear that his mission had been to fuck me into a coma and his success was evident to me by the fight I was having with keeping my eyes open.

"T-thank you, baby," I murmured, willingly folding into the embrace he pulled me into.

I didn't even hear his response because I was already in a land beyond time and space. My sleep started out peaceful and the rest was much needed, but it didn't last. My dreams came in flashes, but the feeling of darkness and doom was inescapable, causing me to toss and turn until finally I gave up on the idea of sleep. I could tell the sun was rising because of the orange glow coming from the curtains, but I didn't immediately get up.

Something was wrong. I could feel it as sure as I could the nigga sleeping beside me. When I'd been a little girl, I'd had nightmares because of my love for scary movies, but my mom would always comfort me by saying it wasn't real. As I got older, I realized what real evil was, but I still saw nightmares as warnings against the things we had yet to see. Something was wrong. I may not have known what was wrong, but I knew I'd have to adapt on the fly so now was the time to finalize a plan in my mind.

Careful not to wake Bone, I got up and hopped in the shower, hoping the water would soothe me and allow my brain a moment to restart. Today was the real first day of forever and I needed to have my third eye open if I was gonna survive.

"Babe," Bone said, knocking on the door.

"It's not locked," I called out.

I heard him open the door and I pulled the shower curtain back, hoping to entice him into joining me, but the look on his face wasn't sexual.

"What is it?"

"Your phone was ringing. It's the senator," he said passing it to me. I saw the three missed calls and I called back.

"I've done what you asked," Senator Jordan said, answering on the first ring.

"Where is he?"

"He'll be released from Big Sandy Federal Prison in Kentucky at eight a.m.," he replied.

"Have him taken to Louisville International Airport and there will be a plane waiting for him. Once he's airborne, your son will be released."

"How do I know you'll release PJ?"

"You don't, but you can bet his life that if you don't do what I say, parts of him will show up on the midafternoon news report," I replied hanging up.

"It's done?" Bone asked.

At this point I didn't trust myself not to breakdown into hysterical crying if I said the words aloud, so I simply nodded my head yes and leaped into his arms. I wouldn't let the tears fall until I could physically touch my father, but I could at least breathe a little easier knowing he'd be on his way in a short time.

"What do we gotta do?" Bone asked, sitting me on my feet and passing me a towel.

"The first thing we gotta do is send a plane to Louisville because he'll be there in a few hours. While I'm doing that, I need you to charter the other plane and have them ready to leave a.s.a.p."

"Moscow?" he asked.

"Just for the time being. Do you have enough money off shore to last for a while?"

The look he gave me told me that was a dumb question. So, I left it alone and went into the bedroom to get dressed. Hurriedly, I threw on the pants and t-shirt I'd had on and got down to the business of arranging my father's transport. Bone went outside to make his phone calls, and when he came back, he had Destiny and Black Sam with him.

"Who's got eyes on the kid?" I asked, knowing now was not the time for anything to happen to him.

"Big Baby's with him," Destiny replied.

I immediately zeroed in on her because her tone was all wrong. In my brief moment of happiness and preparation to celebrate, I'd forgot about my bad dreams and the unsettling feeling that accompanied them. Looking into my sister's face, it all came back, and before she could open her mouth to speak, I was hit with a lightning bolt of sight.

"Where's Angel?" I asked calmly. Her eyes told me I'd hit the nail on the head and the quivering of her lip gave me an indication of how bad it was.

"Free I-"

"Just tell me what happened, Destiny."

"Something went wrong last night and she got shot in the leg, but she was okay. I talked to her, but she promised me she was okay."

"So, where is she?" I asked, fighting to keep my anger in check at being kept out of the loop on something so serious.

"She- I had told her to get back up here a.s.a.p. so she was gonna fly straight back up here, but-but shit got crazy at the Burger King before she could get to the airport."

"The fuck you mean shit got crazy?" I asked growing more fearful and getting kick-ass mad.

"The way it looks is that some nigga tried to hit Deuce and she shot through the Burger King window at them."

"Destiny, where the fuck is our sister."

"She-she got arrested."

Chapter Nineteen
Freedom

It felt like my thoughts were travelling at the speed of light because I'd already done the math on this whole situation. For Angel to catch another body this soon after the shit that had gone down in Atlanta was unreal. The state of Tennessee was gonna try to knock her fucking melon off. And the shit couldn't have come at a worse time because we were all about to be on the run in a couple hours. When I looked at Bone, I could see he was processing the situation just like I was, which meant he was drawing the same conclusion. We were fucked.

"What do I do?" I asked him, needing an answer that would give all of us a way out. He sat down next to me and took my hand in his.

"You've gotta choose, babe. If you stay here and help Angel fight, you might find yourself behind bars because you know the senator is gonna move the earth to find his son's kidnappers. If you kill the boy, it only gets worse. Option B is that you go on the run with your dad and help Angel fight from wherever you land. Your money is long enough for that. Whatever decision you make, I'm with you," he said, squeezing my hand.

I felt like both options were impossible and I was torn in a way I never had been. I was no good to my sister behind bars, but was I any good to her halfway around the world?

"We might be able to get Angel out before dad if-"

"Dad is being released in a hour," I said, looking at my phone.

"W-what?" Destiny replied.

I looked at her and nodded my head with a sad smile. We'd waited so long and worked so hard for this moment, but in life, fate can move the process on a chess board quicker and more efficient than you can. I knew I had to make a decision, but making the wrong one would hurt me forever. When I looked at Bone, the love and loyalty was blatant in his eyes, and that forced another truth for me to consider. Our child.

"I can't make this decision alone, you have to give me your input," I told him.

"Well, neither of us wants our baby born in a prison or growing up without you."

"Hold up? What baby?" Destiny asked loudly.

I ignored her and kept looking into his eyes, listening to the truth in his words, and taking comfort in the fact that he'd be with me no matter what.

"Big Baby is someone we can trust, right?" I asked, looking at Destiny.

"Yeah."

"Then we gotta make sure he's willing to do everything he can for Angel until we can get her out."

"Free, what are you saying?" she asked.

"I'm saying too much has been done to undo it now. I'm saying we gotta run or risk the whole family ending up behind bars," I replied sullenly.

I didn't like the idea any more than she did, but neither of us could argue with the truth.

"Black Sam, no one knows you were involved, but I still want you to come with us because we're definitely gonna need your help," I said.

"As long as I can leave of my own free will whenever I want."

"Agreed," I replied.

"The plane is being fueled now," Bone said.

It seriously hurt my heart to know that I had to leave Angel behind because that was something we swore to never do. If I didn't, though, I'd be giving up my father, my sister, and my freedom.

"We've got a lot to do and only a little time to do it. Destiny, I want you to tell Big Baby and Lil Boy to load PJ into the truck because they're gonna drive him back to Delaware. Don't look at me like that because that's the last place anybody would be looking for him. The truck is untraceable, or at least it'll never come back to us, so once I call them, they can leave him in the truck and I'll tell his daddy where to find him. Make sure the truck is wiped down ahead of time, make sure they wear gloves, and make sure they blindfold him. One of them needs to follow the other in Bone's truck so they can get away afterwards, okay?"

"I'll go tell them now," she replied, turning around to leave.

"Black Sam, we're gonna be taking a flight soon and the moment that plane is in the air, I need all the records of flight manifests or flight plans to disappear like they never existed. Cool?"

"Not a problem," she replied.

"Put your shit in Destiny's car because we're leaving soon," I told her.

Once she was gone, Bone and I set about erasing our existence from the motel room as quickly as we could. By the time I got the message that my father was in route to the airport, we were all packed up and ready to make the last leg of the journey. Both Destiny and I got emotional when saying goodbye to Big Baby and Lil Boy, partly because we were gonna miss them, and partly because we knew they'd be our only link to Angel for a while. They promised to look after her and do everything we asked, which didn't take away the guilt I felt, but it made it bearable.

Flying out from a private plane made your airport experience easier, but it was still an hour before we were all aboard our G4, waiting for my father's G3 to land. On the ride to the airport, I'd gotten the text that my father was in the air and once it was verified with a picture taken at thirty-seven-thousand feet up, I told the senator where to find his son. With that business conducted, my phone had become nothing more than pieces of plastic as it disintegrated from direct contact with the highway. Unfortunately, that almost meant I had no way of knowing how long I had to wait for his plane to land, and I was beyond anxious.

"Everything is gonna be alright," Bone said, passing me a much-needed glass of Hennessy. It was halfway to my mouth before I thought about my baby and quickly put it down.

"It's just coke," he said, smiling.

I appreciated him trying to lighten the mood, even though he wasn't successful.

"Sir, there's a G3 taxiing into our hanger now," the pilot said over the intercom.

I locked eyes with Destiny and I knew she probably saw the same fear in mine as I did in hers. I stood up and she followed me off the plane where we waited for the other jet to complete its turnaround in the hanger so it would be facing the runway again. It seemed like forever until the door opened and the staircase was lowered. And then there he was. I'd heard people say things like "if I'm dreaming don't wake me up," but it wasn't until this moment that I completely understood how they felt. My dream was coming true before my very eyes and he never looked more alive.

"Daddy," we squealed in unison, running to him. I could see the tears already on his face before we were swept up into his arms the way he used to when we were little girls.

"My babies, my precious babies," he said, kissing us and squeezing the breath from us before he put us down.

"Come on, we gotta go," I said, grabbing him by the hand.

"Wait, where's Angel?" he asked looking around.

I'd really hoped to avoid this question, but there was no scenario in life where I saw that happening.

"I'll explain on the plane. But, dad, we gotta go," I persisted, still trying to pull him.

"We can't go."

"What?" I asked, looking at him like he was crazy.

"We can't run, Freedom. I don't know what story they fed you about why I was transferred and cut off from all communication, but it was a lie. They tried to bury me because I found out the truth."

"What truth?" Destiny asked.

"The truth about your mom…and how she's still alive."

To Be Continued...
The Boss Man's Daughters 2
Available Now!

Stay Connected with Us!

Text **LOCKDOWN** to 22828 to stay up-to-date with new releases, sneak peaks, contests and more…

Thank you!

Submission Guideline.

Submit the first three chapters of your completed manuscript to ldpsubmissions@gmail.com, subject line: Your book's title. The manuscript must be in a .doc file and sent as an attachment. Document should be in Times New Roman, double spaced and in size 12 font. Also, provide your synopsis and full contact information. If sending multiple submissions, they must each be in a separate email.

Have a story but no way to send it electronically? You can still submit to LDP/Ca$h Presents. Send in the first three chapters, written or typed, of your completed manuscript to:

LDP: Submissions Dept
Po Box 870494
Mesquite, Tx 75187

DO NOT send original manuscript. Must be a duplicate.

Provide your synopsis and a cover letter containing your full contact information.

Thanks for considering LDP and Ca$h Presents.

Coming Soon from Lock Down Publications/Ca$h Presents

BOW DOWN TO MY GANGSTA

By **Ca$h**

TORN BETWEEN TWO

By **Coffee**

BLOOD STAINS OF A SHOTTA **II**

By **Jamaica**

WHEN THE STREETS CLAP BACK **II**

By **Jibril Williams**

STEADY MOBBIN

By **Marcellus Allen**

BLOOD OF A BOSS **V**

By **Askari**

BRIDE OF A HUSTLA **III**

By **Destiny Skai**

WHEN A GOOD GIRL GOES BAD **II**

By **Adrienne**

LOVE & CHASIN' PAPER **II**

By **Qay Crockett**

THE HEART OF A GANGSTA **III**

By **Jerry Jackson**

LOYAL TO THE GAME **IV**

By **T.J. & Jelissa**

A DOPEBOY'S PRAYER **II**

By **Eddie "Wolf" Lee**

IF LOVING YOU IS WRONG… **III**

By **Jelissa**

BLOODY COMMAS **III**

SKI MASK CARTEL II

By **T.J. Edwards**

BLAST FOR ME **II**

RAISED AS A GOON V

BRED BY THE SLUMS

By **Ghost**

A DISTINGUISHED THUG STOLE MY HEART **III**

By **Meesha**

ADDICTIED TO THE DRAMA **II**

By **Jamila Mathis**

LIPSTICK KILLAH II

By **Mimi**

THE BOSSMAN'S DAUGHTERS 4

By **Aryanna**

Available Now

RESTRAINING ORDER **I & II**

By **CA$H & Coffee**

LOVE KNOWS NO BOUNDARIES **I II & III**

By **Coffee**

RAISED AS A GOON I, II, III & IV

By **Ghost**

LAY IT DOWN **I & II**

LAST OF A DYING BREED

BLOOD STAINS OF A SHOTTA

By **Jamaica**

LOYAL TO THE GAME

LOYAL TO THE GAME II

LOYAL TO THE GAME III

By **TJ & Jelissa**

BLOODY COMMAS I & II

SKI MASK CARTEL

By **T.J. Edwards**

IF LOVING HIM IS WRONG…I & II

By **Jelissa**

WHEN THE STREETS CLAP BACK

By **Jibril Williams**

A DISTINGUISHED THUG STOLE MY HEART I & II

By **Meesha**

PUSH IT TO THE LIMIT

By **Bre' Hayes**

BLOOD OF A BOSS **I, II, III & IV**

By **Askari**

THE STREETS BLEED MURDER **I, II & III**

THE HEART OF A GANGSTA I & II

By **Jerry Jackson**

CUM FOR ME

CUM FOR ME 2

CUM FOR ME 3

An **LDP Erotica Collaboration**

BRIDE OF A HUSTLA **I & II**

THE FETTI GIRLS **I, II& III**

By **Destiny Skai**

WHEN A GOOD GIRL GOES BAD

By **Adrienne**

A GANGSTER'S REVENGE **I II III & IV**

THE BOSS MAN'S DAUGHTERS

THE BOSS MAN'S DAUGHTERS II

THE BOSSMAN'S DAUGHTERS III

A SAVAGE LOVE **I & II**

BAE BELONGS TO ME

A HUSTLER'S DECEIT I, II

By **Aryanna**

A KINGPIN'S AMBITON

A KINGPIN'S AMBITION **II**

I MURDER FOR THE DOUGH

By **Ambitious**

TRUE SAVAGE

TRUE SAVAGE II

TRUE SAVAGE **III**

By **Chris Green**

A DOPEBOY'S PRAYER

By **Eddie "Wolf" Lee**

THE KING CARTEL **I, II & III**

By **Frank Gresham**

THESE NIGGAS AIN'T LOYAL **I, II & III**

By **Nikki Tee**

GANGSTA SHYT **I II &III**

By **CATO**

THE ULTIMATE BETRAYAL

By **Phoenix**

BOSS'N UP **I , II & III**

By **Royal Nicole**

I LOVE YOU TO DEATH

By Destiny J

I RIDE FOR MY HITTA

I STILL RIDE FOR MY HITTA

By **Misty Holt**

LOVE & CHASIN' PAPER

By **Qay Crockett**

TO DIE IN VAIN

By **ASAD**

BROOKLYN HUSTLAZ

By **Boogsy Morina**

BROOKLYN ON LOCK I & II

By **Sonovia**

GANGSTA CITY

By **Teddy Duke**

A DRUG KING AND HIS DIAMOND

A DOPEMAN'S RICHES

By Nicole Goosby

BOOKS BY LDP'S CEO, CA$H

TRUST IN NO MAN

TRUST IN NO MAN 2

TRUST IN NO MAN 3

BONDED BY BLOOD

SHORTY GOT A THUG

THUGS CRY

THUGS CRY 2

THUGS CRY 3

TRUST NO BITCH

TRUST NO BITCH 2

TRUST NO BITCH 3

TIL MY CASKET DROPS

RESTRAINING ORDER

RESTRAINING ORDER 2

IN LOVE WITH A CONVICT

Coming Soon

BONDED BY BLOOD 2

BOW DOWN TO MY GANGSTA

CPSIA information can be obtained
at www.ICGtesting.com
Printed in the USA
LVHW081317130821
695242LV00020B/520